THE
UNCERTAIN
JOURNEY

Books by **Margaret Poynter**

A Time Too Swift

What's One More?

Under the High Seas
(with Donald Collins)

Cosmic Quest
(with Michael J. Klein)

THE UNCERTAIN JOURNEY

Stories of Illegal Aliens in *El Norte*

MARGARET POYNTER
illustrated with photographs

Atheneum   1992   New York
Maxwell Macmillan Canada
TORONTO
Maxwell Macmillan International
NEW YORK   OXFORD   SINGAPORE   SYDNEY

Copyright © 1992 by Margaret Poynter
All rights reserved. No part of this book may be reproduced
or transmitted in any form or by any means, electronic or
mechanical, including photocopying, recording, or by any
information storage and retrieval system, without permission
in writing from the Publisher.
Atheneum
Macmillan Publishing Company
866 Third Avenue
New York, NY 10022
Maxwell Macmillan Canada, Inc.
1200 Eglinton Avenue East
Suite 200
Don Mills, Ontario M3C 3N1
Macmillan Publishing Company is part of the
Maxwell Communication Group of Companies.

First edition
Printed in the United States of America
10 9 8 7 6 5 4 3 2 1
The text of this book is set in 11 pt. Bembo.
Designed by Kimberly M. Adlerman

Library of Congress Cataloging-in-Publication Data
Poynter, Margaret.
The uncertain journey: stories of illegal aliens in el Norte/by
Margaret Poynter; illustrated with photographs.—1st ed.
p.   cm.
Summary: Tells the stories of twelve South Americans, Central
Americans, Mexicans, and Caribbean Islanders who entered the United
States to work as illegal aliens and overcame many physical and
financial ordeals.
ISBN 0–689–31623–2
1. Aliens, Illegal—United States—Juvenile literature.
[1. Aliens, Illegal.   2. United States—Emigration and immigration.]
I. Title.
JV6455.5.P69   1992
325.73—dc20   91–8857

To Arnulfo, for having the
courage to undertake
the uncertain journey and
for being *mi amigo*

CONTENTS

Sin Papeles 1
1. The Eyes and Ears of *La Migra* . . . 13
2. *Adios, Mi Niños* 26
3. *No Problema* 36
4. How Long Is a Row? 54
5. If You Want Your Children . . . 66
6. You Are Only a Boy 75
7. The *Bot Pipple* 84
8. He Will Give Me Sanctuary 95
9. The Desert Will Bite You, Scratch You, or Poison You 106
10. The Darkness Hides the *Banditos* 124
11. You Will Never Work as I Have Worked 136
12. I Want to Help You 149
I Have Survived! 160
Bibliography 163

THE
UNCERTAIN
JOURNEY

Sin Papeles

They clear the tables, wash the dishes, and mop the floors of our restaurants. They wash our cars, manufacture our clothing, do our laundry, dig our ditches, and man our factory assembly lines. They plant and harvest our crops, mow our lawns, and toil in our canneries and fish-packing plants. They stand on our street corners selling fruit or offering to shine our shoes.

To get these menial, tedious, low-paying, often physically grueling jobs, these men and women walk, crawl, and swim across our southern border, facing hardships and dangers in the darkness of night. They come from such impoverished countries as Mexico, Guatemala, Colombia, and Haiti, where at least half of them live in dirt-floored hovels with no plumbing or electricity. Only a few understand English; most of them can't read or write their native language. The jobs they find here are dreams come true. The money they earn may make the difference between whether their children remain uneducated or go to

THE UNCERTAIN JOURNEY

school. It may even determine whether those children will live or will die from lack of food and medical care.

They are the tens of thousands of *sin papeles,* "those without papers," who enter the United States illegally every year.

Before the start of this century, there was no such thing as an illegal alien in the United States. All immigrants were welcomed because our young, growing country needed people to work in our factories and to farm our vast expanse of empty land. Then, as our cities grew crowded, and our good farmland scarce, laws were passed to control the number of people who were allowed to become legal residents, and thus, to take jobs. To enforce those laws, the United States Immigration and Naturalization Service (INS) was created. The United States Border Patrol is the "police force" of the INS. Its officers have the job of apprehending illegal aliens as they attempt to enter our country.

Most of the people who enter the United States illegally are Mexicans. For them, getting into *El Norte* is just a matter of walking or swimming across a largely unprotected border. Salvadorans, Colombians, and Jamaicans, however, usually hire a *coyote,* a smuggler of people, to provide transportation and guidance. In the plazas, bus depots, and coffee shops of their countries, the *pollos,* "chickens" or "those who run," make contact with *coyotes.* Money changes hands, and a time and place of departure is arranged.

Most *coyotes* are honest, with a handshake guaranteeing

─────────────── Sin Papeles ───────────────

the eventual success of their mission. However, the possibility of dealing with a dishonest *coyote* is the first hazard many illegal aliens must face. Some *pollos* have been stranded in life-threatening situations, and smugglers sometimes extort more money from their former clients by threatening to report them to *la migra,* someone who works for the immigration service.

Because of the numbers of men and women who look to *El Norte* as the answer to their pressing problems, *coyotes* do a brisk business. Some of them work individually, recruiting a few people at a time. Others belong to a far-flung network of smugglers who contract with the owners of large ranches and farms to furnish crews of workers.

The *coyote* networks are remarkably efficient. Several years ago, the border patrol started using helicopters in the area between Tijuana, Mexico, and San Ysidro, California. Within a week, *coyotes* in Quito, Ecuador, were telling their clients how to avoid being spotted by the aircrafts' searchlights.

There's a border patrol checkpoint twenty miles to the north of San Diego, California, but there isn't enough money or manpower to keep it open twenty-four hours a day. The *coyotes* post lookouts to signal when it is safe to transport their *pollos.* Two minutes after the checkpoint closes, vans and trucks that have been parked a few miles south are being loaded up and are on their way to Los Angeles.

The border patrol is familiar with the *coyotes*' strategy. They often know the names of most of the lookouts and what shifts they are working.

THE UNCERTAIN JOURNEY

Since the border patrol and the illegal aliens are on opposing sides in an ongoing war, there have been some violent confrontations between them. Usually, though, they are friendly enemies. As a border patrol agent takes his busload of illegal aliens to a port of entry where they will walk back across the border into Mexico, he knows that at least half of his prisoners will try to return to the United States within twenty-four hours. *"Adios, amigo,"* the deportees may say to their captor. "Next time, we will be more careful."

"I'll be watching for you," says the border patrol officer with a smile.

In one case, two border patrolmen got their car stuck in the sand on the northern side of the border. "Can you give us a hand?" they called to two Mexican youths standing on the opposite riverbank. Without question, the boys swam across the river, helped the patrolmen out of their predicament, then returned to Mexico.

"I have a lot of respect for the people who come here looking for work," said one border patrol officer. "What other choice do they have? But still, it's my job to catch as many of them as I can."

The fact is, though, that only one out of every five illegal aliens is caught at the border, and only half of the alarms set off by the border patrol's electronic sensors are responded to. "There are just too many of them [the illegals] and not enough of us," said an immigration official. "Only about thirty miles of our two-thousand-mile border is fenced. To do our job right, there would have to be

Sin Papeles

an officer standing every few feet, twenty-four hours a day along the entire border."

Once a *sin papeles* is in the United States, there is little chance he will be caught by the immigration service. He may simply take a bus to the nearest city where he will disappear into the crowds, or he may walk to a nearby farming community. In many cases, a *coyote* will have arranged to transport him in a van or a truck, or, less often, on a late-night airplane flight to a prearranged job site.

Most immigrants are heading for California, Texas, Arizona, and Florida, but they may end up working in the garment district of New York, the stockyards of Chicago, or the fields and orchards of Michigan and Oregon.

To most Mexicans, being deported is nothing but an inconvenience. The trip back from their country may be hazardous, but it is one that is easily made again and again. But to Ecuadorans or Hondurans, who may have sold all their possessions and also gone into debt for their trip to the United States, deportation means that they will return home to face even worse poverty than they endured before they left. The fear of *la migra* remains with them every minute they are in this country.

In some cases, this ever-present fear is compounded by the fact that imprisonment or death may await the deportee when he or she returns to his or her homeland. Thousands of Haitians fled to Florida when their lives were threatened by a tyrannical dictator. The unstable governments of some Central American countries cause citizens

THE UNCERTAIN JOURNEY

to be favored by the rulers one month, only to find that they are objects of persecution the next. Such situations have caused thousands of Guatemalans and Salvadorans to flee to the United States. If they are caught by the INS, they may be able to avoid deportation if they can prove that they are political refugees. Unfortunately, such proof is hard to come by.

After a *sin papeles* enters the United States, he is a stranger in an often hostile land. An unscrupulous employer can easily victimize a desperate man or woman who is willing to take a job no matter how low the pay or how poor the working conditions. Most *sin papeles* are afraid to open a bank account, because to do so means leaving a record of their presence in this country. They are also unwilling to leave their money in their dwelling places because if they are deported, they may not be given time to collect their belongings. As a result, many of them carry large amounts of money in their wallets, making them an attractive target for thieves.

Several illegal immigrants may pool their money to pay a month's rent on an apartment. A dishonest landlord, after collecting his money in advance, may report his tenants to the INS. After their capture, he will repeat the procedure again and again, making many times the profit he would make if he were honest.

An illegal immigrant's fear of *la migra* extends to anyone who wears a uniform or is in any way connected to the government. If he is robbed, he is afraid to report the crime to the police. If he is cheated by an employer, a

Sin Papeles

landlord, or a merchant, he is afraid to file a complaint with the proper agency. If he needs medical help, he hesitates to seek treatment from a doctor or a hospital.

Most *sin papeles* come from a culture where family ties are supremely important, and all but a few of them must leave their families behind. As months turn into years of separation, the emotional pain they suffer is tremendous.

These and many other factors combine to overwhelm the *sin papeles* as they try to cope with life in *El Norte*. Fortunately, their plight is eased by many churches, social service agencies, and volunteer groups that give counseling, legal advice, food, and shelter to thousands of illegal aliens every day. This help may represent the only support the immigrants receive as they strive for a better life.

To the *sin papeles,* the hope of getting a job in the United States far outweighs any possible problems they may face. As long as the situation in their homelands is hopeless, they will continue to seek work in *El Norte*.

It's estimated that there are one to three million illegal aliens in the United States at any one time. Many citizens object to this situation.

"They're taking away jobs that belong to us," says an unemployed mechanic.

The fact is that most undocumented, or illegal, workers have only a second-grade education and very few job skills. As a result, they are happy to take the jobs that most Americans don't want or will take only temporarily. Farmers, restaurant owners, and clothing manufacturers would have a difficult time staying in business without the *sin papeles*. Some economists have gone so far as to say that the economy of some states—California, for one—would grind to a halt if all of the undocumented workers suddenly disappeared.

"Illegal aliens don't pay their fair share of taxes," says a grocery store clerk.

Like many American citizens who are unable to find full-time employment, illegal aliens are often paid in cash by people who hire them for gardening or paving a driveway or building a wall. Those who have found more permanent jobs, however, have federal, state, and other taxes deducted from their checks. The big difference between them and the legal residents is that most illegal aliens probably won't be in this country long enough to collect any overpayment on their income tax or to reap any benefits from the money they have contributed to Social Security.

"But their children are going to school here," a mother of three complains. "Aren't we paying for their education?"

Only a small percentage of *sin papeles* bring their children with them. Also, any illegal alien who lives in a house or an apartment pays rent, part of which is used for the landlord's property taxes, which support our schools. One problem that does arise wherever there are non-English-speaking children attending school is that of communication. Many classes in the Los Angeles, California, school system must be conducted in both English and Spanish. This bilingual education costs more than teaching in only one language.

"Illegal aliens send most of their money home," says the

owner of a market. "Since they don't spend it here, our own business people are suffering."

It's true that undocumented workers send a large share of their wages to their families back home. It's also true that hundreds of clothing stores, markets, and places of entertainment have come into existence just to serve the needs of the great numbers of Hispanic and Caribbean immigrants. These businesses contribute to the economic health of their communities. Still, many economists issue warnings about the dangers of a "money drain" from the United States into foreign countries.

"If all these foreigners keep coming, someday they will outnumber us," says a retired army officer.

Many people are concerned about the fact that the number of immigrants, both legal and illegal, has increased dramatically during the past twenty years. Some of them resent having any language but English used in our schools and businesses and polling places. They are frightened at the changes that people from other cultures have brought with them.

But, reply historians, almost all of our not too distant ancestors came from somewhere else. Our current society is a result of the blending of these many diverse cultures. Eventually, as in the past, "they," the immigrants we fear today, will be absorbed into our communities and will become "us," accepted members of our society.

Sin papeles know little about the problems or benefits they bring to the United States. As long as there are no jobs in their countries and there is work to be found here,

THE UNCERTAIN JOURNEY

they will continue to cross our border, and the INS will continue to do everything in its power to catch them. To offset a lack of money and manpower, our immigration officials consider any idea that may help them do their job more efficiently. One suggestion has been to build a wall along our entire southern border. It was decided that such a structure would be too expensive to construct and to maintain.

The busiest illegal alien entry point is located just a few miles south of San Diego, California. Recently, a string of powerful floodlights was erected on the levees along that portion of the border. Few *sin papeles* have been deterred. They simply cross outside the circle of illumination.

Several years ago, someone suggested that a deep, wide ditch be dug just north of the border running in an east-west direction across the California-Arizona deserts. This idea was never seriously considered. Besides doing damage to the fragile ecology of that area, the project would be very expensive.

The Immigration Reform and Control Act of 1986 was the most far-reaching plan ever put into effect to stem the flow of illegal aliens into the United States. One aim of the program was to give millions of undocumented workers who were already established here the chance to apply for amnesty and be free of the fear of deportation. Eventually, after learning basic English and taking courses in United States history and government, they could become legal residents and even citizens.

The second aim was to make it impossible for illegal aliens to find jobs. This goal was to be accomplished

Sin Papeles

by punishing the employers who hired undocumented workers.

For over two years after the amnesty program went into effect, there was a decrease in the number of people illegally entering our country. Then, as amnesty applicants become temporary legal residents, many of them sent for their families. Also, many *sin papeles* bought false papers and presented them to their prospective employers. Since the employers weren't required to verify the papers, undocumented workers were still being hired.

By 1990 there were just as many people entering our country illegally as there had been before 1986. It had become evident that the amnesty law was a failure. There was talk of hiring more border patrol officers and of supplying them with more helicopters, planes, jeeps, and horses; of putting up more walls and fences; and of installing more lights. The problem with all of these measures, though, is that they don't change the fact that the United States is an irresistible magnet to the poverty-stricken people south of our border.

"They will continue to come, no matter what," said the administrator of a migrant shelter in Tijuana, Mexico. "The United States could build a moat and fill it with sharks and crocodiles, but they will still find a way to cross the border."

Some of our own government officials agree that any attempt to keep out the *sin papeles* is doomed to failure, that the holes in our leaky southern border can never be effectively plugged. They are in favor of having an open border, over which people can come and go at will.

THE UNCERTAIN JOURNEY

"We need the workers, and the workers need us," they argue. "Don't punish them just for trying to earn a living."

The *sin papeles* know they are breaking the law when they enter the United States illegally. The fact that they are considered criminals, however, is unimportant compared to the fact that *El Norte* represents their only hope of survival. They must work or their families will starve.

Here are the stories of some of the men and women who have experienced the hardships and the dangers involved with *la lucha,* the fight, an outlaw trip into a foreign land, the uncertain passage.

"Me defendi," each says with pride. "I have survived!"

1

The Eyes and Ears of *La Migra*...

Ricardo will always remember the exact moment that he decided to go to the United States. He was seventeen and was sitting with his friend, Pedro, on a rickety bench pushed against the outside wall of his family's two-room adobe house in the Mexican city of Cepeda.

"Let's go to *El Norte*," he had said.

"The very same thought was in my head," Pedro had replied.

Both boys had been working in a *huarachario*, a small shoe factory that had recently shut down. Now, there was no work to be found in all of Cepeda. By walking to the nearby towns, they could occasionally make a dollar or two building a fence or digging a ditch, but such work was scarce, and when it was over, the job search had to begin again.

When Ricardo's father had been alive, there had always been enough food on the table. Since his death, the main meal for Ricardo, his mother, and his younger brother and

THE UNCERTAIN JOURNEY

sister was often only a tortilla wrapped around some beans.

Pedro's father was still alive, but tuberculosis had weakened him so much that he was often unable to leave his bed to work his small farm. Besides Pedro, there were five other children in the family. When necessary, even the six-year-old worked in the field, but there was never enough money to buy shoes for everyone.

It was not enough to say, "Let's go to *El Norte.*" Neither boy knew how to get to the border or how to cross it undetected by the United States Border Patrol. The next day, they walked the fifteen miles to the home of Pedro's uncle, who had made the trip north many times.

Two hours after their arrival, the boys left with suggestions on how to ward off the dangers and ease the hardships of the journey. They also had a loan of one hundred dollars, a crudely drawn map of the route they were to take, and the address of a cousin in San Antonio, Texas.

Three days later, after receiving a blessing from Ricardo's tearful mother, the boys left Cepeda.

For over a week, they walked the dusty roads of the villages and the paved streets of the larger towns, making their way northward, sleeping only when exhaustion forced them to stop, eating only when hunger caused their steps to falter.

As the sun was setting on the tenth day, they stood on the banks of the Rio Bravo, the last barrier that separated them from the riches they hoped to find in the United States. As he stared at the water, Ricardo recalled the words of Pedro's uncle. "In the river, there are fish with

The Eyes and Ears of La Migra . . .

sharp teeth who may bite you in the stomach. And the river—it swirls around and drags you to the bottom, like it's trying to gobble you up. Don't swim too strongly. Go with the water, not against it.

"And be sure to cross at night, silently, when a cloud covers the face of the moon. The eyes and ears of *la migra* could be anywhere."

As the boys waited for darkness, men and women and a few children gathered along the riverbank. Muted conversations, the scuttering of lizards, and the chirping of birds were all that disturbed the silence. Finally, about an hour after sunset, the first *sin papeles* slid down the steeply sloping bank and entered the water. Two others soon followed, then three more who had brought inflated inner tubes with them. A man and a woman, each with a child sitting on their shoulders, were next. Another family pushed the overturned hood of an old car into the water, then clambered aboard and, using boards as paddles, made their way toward the opposite riverbank.

Emboldened by the courage of the others, Ricardo and Pedro joined them in the water. For a few moments, Ricardo felt the hard roundness of stones beneath his feet, but suddenly the river bottom fell away and he was being swept downstream. His first instinct was to battle the current, then he recalled the advice of Pedro's uncle. Slowly, stroke by stroke, he and Pedro made their way to the opposite riverbank. Five minutes later, they emerged several hundred yards downstream from where they had entered the water. For a moment, they knelt to give thanks to the Virgin Mary for their own safe crossing and for the safe crossing of everyone else who had challenged the river that night.

That moment was all it took to be spotted by two border patrolmen who had been alerted when an electronic detection device had been tripped by one of the *sin papeles*. As Ricardo and Pedro rose from their short prayer, they were blinded by the headlights of a jeep that was bearing down upon them. Both boys ran to the riverbank and jumped back into the water. In their haste, they left the plastic bags that contained their food and change of clothing. Fortunately, they had pinned their money inside their shirts.

There was no need for silence now. Splashing, kicking, gasping for breath, they swam back to Mexico. After making their way to a border town, they bought some more food and rummaged through trash cans to find two plastic bottles which they would later fill with water from the Rio Bravo.

At midnight, Ricardo and Pedro again plunged into the treacherous waters of the river. As soon as they stepped onto the soil of the United States, they dashed into the brush and sat there like rocks, barely breathing, listening for any sign that their arrival had been detected. But there was nothing but the ordinary sounds of the night—the chirping of crickets, the rush of water, the drone of an airplane engine from somewhere far away. Furtively, the boys stood up and began their long journey to San Antonio, following the highway, throwing themselves behind bushes or rolling into a ditch whenever a vehicle ap-

The Eyes and Ears of La Migra . . .

proached them, praying that they would not land in a nest of rattlesnakes, whose bite is much worse than that of *la migra.*

On the second day after the river crossing, Ricardo spotted a man sprawled on the sand near a clump of cactus. He and Pedro ran toward him, hoping they could help him, but they were too late. The man's water bottle was half full, and nearby there was an unopened package of tortillas, so he had not died of hunger or thirst. It was Pedro who noticed the small punctures on his swollen arm, evidence that the man had fallen victim to a snake.

Despite the danger of being spotted by *la migra,* the boys used their hands to scoop out enough sand to form a shallow grave. Before burying the man, they went through his pockets, hoping to find a paper with a name and address on it. There was no such paper. His fate would never be known to the people who loved him.

The dead man had no more use for his food and water, so the boys took them. Still, their supplies ran out on the morning of the fourth day. They had to rely on springs for their water, and on certain cactus plants, which Pedro's uncle had said were safe to eat, for their food. Late that afternoon, some farm workers, no doubt *sin papeles* like themselves, filled their plastic bottles with water and gave them some bread.

The next day, Ricardo developed blisters on his feet, and both he and Pedro had become ill from the sun. They were so weak that they did not try to run when a man in a jeep approached them. "Hello," the man said in the language of Mexico. "Where are you going?"

THE UNCERTAIN JOURNEY

"San Antonio," Pedro replied.

The man laughed. "Well, from the looks of you, you're not going to make it. I can use some help on my ranch for a while." He motioned for them to get into his jeep.

The boys knew they might be walking into a trap, but they were too exhausted to refuse the offer. They had, after all, been offered a job, and finding work was the reason they had come to the United States. Fortunately, the man was exactly who he appeared to be—a rancher who needed some help. For a week, Ricardo and Pedro worked ten hours a day mending fences, stacking hay, and cleaning cattle barns. Ricardo felt blessed. He had survived the hazards of the river and the desert. He had escaped *la migra*. And he had found a job by which he could earn the money to continue his journey to San Antonio.

But on the eighth day, Ricardo spotted an official-looking car driving along the road that bordered the north side of the ranch. The car stopped, and the driver got out and talked to the ranch owner. *La migra!* Ricardo thought. He ran to find Pedro, who was working in one of the barns.

"Hide!" he said, breathlessly. Both boys climbed up the ladder that led to the loft and burrowed under the hay. Twenty minutes later, Ricardo heard the voice of the ranch owner and that of a stranger as they walked through the door of the barn. "See, no one here," said the ranch owner. "Come with me, and you can meet my workers. They showed me their papers. They're legal."

Ricardo and Pedro didn't come down from the hayloft for another twenty minutes, then they crept down the

The Eyes and Ears of La Migra . . .

ladder, ready to run if they heard anyone coming. After staying in the barn until nightfall, they walked to their bunkhouse. The next morning, they told the ranch owner they wanted to move on to San Antonio. "In the city, it will be easier to hide from *la migra*," Ricardo said. "Besides, Pedro's cousin is expecting us to come."

"I understand," the ranch owner said. "Finish out the day, and I'll give you your pay in the morning. Maybe I can even give you a ride into San Antonio." He paused. "Probably just as well you're leaving. Those immigration guys will be back, and the next time, they might find you."

By seven o'clock the next morning, Ricardo and Pedro had been fed a big breakfast and been given fifty dollars apiece for their labor. When it was time for them to leave, one of the Mexican ranch hands drove up in a jeep. "Climb in," he said. "I'll drop you off half a mile outside the city. There are a lot of immigration people in San Antonio, and I might get stopped and accused of being a *coyote*."

"No problem," said Pedro. "We'll find our way all right."

Almost a month after they had left Cepeda, Ricardo and Pedro were welcomed by Pedro's cousin, Juan, into his small apartment located in the industrial section of the city. When the two boys arrived, there were already six men living in the three-room dwelling. Since some worked days and some worked nights, and they all picked up extra jobs whenever they could, there was always someone leaving for work or coming home from work or making a sandwich or sleeping on one of the mattresses that were scattered on the floor. Despite the confusion, everyone was relaxed and in good humor. Although there was much talk of the families they had left behind, they were all grateful that, for this day at least, they had work to do and they had escaped the watchful eyes of *la migra*.

That night, Ricardo slept on a blanket spread on the floor with his rolled up jeans as a pillow and his jacket as a blanket. The next morning, he and Pedro questioned their roommates about finding work for themselves.

"There's a new construction job starting up about a mile from here," one of the men said. "They'll probably need workers."

"I saw a Help Wanted sign in a restaurant not far from here," said another.

"My work is cleaning offices," said Juan. "I'll ask my boss if he needs anyone."

Within three days, with the help of the "job grapevine," Ricardo had started work on the assembly line of a factory, and Pedro had become a busboy in a restaurant. A month later, that same restaurant had an opening for a dishwasher on the night shift, and Ricardo took on that job also. Now, he had plenty of money to pay his share of the rent and to send money to his parents. When he had paid off his share of the loan from Pedro's uncle, he started going to dances on his night off. He hoped to make new friends—maybe even meet a girl with whom he could share his new life in *El Norte*. A month later, he was introduced to Ana, who seemed to like his company as much as he liked hers.

Ricardo had known Ana only a short time when he went

The Eyes and Ears of La Migra . . .

to work one morning to find the factory gates locked and a sign that read CLOSED in both English and Spanish.

For a few moments, Ricardo dwelled upon his disappointment, then he turned and walked two miles to *el mosca,* a busy intersection where men who needed work waited for people to drive up and offer them jobs. *El mosca* is the Spanish word for fly, and these "hiring corners" got their name because of the way the hopeful workers cluster around the cars like flies cluster around spilled honey. The winners at *el mosca* are the men who are able to grab the door handle of the car and who are also able to do the work that is being offered.

To try to win this prize, Ricardo showed up at the corner every day at 7:00 A.M. One day he was hired, along with two other men, to work on a loading platform; another day, he helped his employer put up a fence; and later in the week, he was employed as a painter's helper. For each of these jobs, he was paid well and at the end of the day was driven back to the hiring corner.

After several days had passed without getting a job, Ricardo was happy to be hired to load chunks of concrete into a truck. For eight hours, Ricardo performed the brutally hard work. At the end of that time, his employer handed him $10, then drove off in the loaded truck, leaving an exhausted Ricardo to find his own way home.

"Me defendi," he told a sympathetic Ana that night. "I survived. The wrong that man does will come back to him in the future."

The next day, two vans pulled up in front of *el mosca* *"Trabajo para todos,"* the drivers called out. "Work for everyone! You, you, you, and you, quick, hop in!" Without any idea of what sort of work they were being offered or where they would be taken, forty men rushed for the seats in the vans. A disappointed Ricardo was left behind when the vehicles pulled away. He didn't find out how lucky he had been until later in the week, when he was told that those vans had belonged to *la migra* and that their passengers had been taken to a detention center, then driven to the border and escorted back into Mexico.

Despite the perils of *el mosca,* Ricardo kept returning at 7:00 A.M. every day except Sunday. The knowledge that an employer might take advantage of him or that he might be caught by *la migra* was overshadowed by the hope that he would be hired for a long-term job. If he hadn't been hired by noon, he searched for work by visiting construction sites, knocking at the back doors of restaurants, and following leads he'd been given by friends. Once, he got a day's work by standing in front of a building supply store and holding a sign offering his services to the customers who were buying construction materials. Meanwhile, because of his job at the restaurant, he was able to pay his rent and to buy his food, but he had only a little left over to send to Mexico.

Finally he found full-time work in a lumberyard, stacking planks and unpacking supplies. He made only two dollars an hour, but his boss paid him promptly. Twice a month, he took his paycheck, cashed it, and bought a money order for the entire amount. The money order was then mailed to his mother, who spent much of it on medical care for Ricardo's brother. Ricardo didn't understand exactly what was wrong with little Felipe, but he knew that his illness was serious.

Because of his concern for Felipe, Ricardo was almost relieved when two immigration officers walked into the back door of the restaurant one night. "I have no green card, no papers," he readily admitted. After spending the rest of the night in a detention center, he was put on a southward-bound bus, and two days later was home. He regretted losing time from work and he missed Ana, but he was overjoyed to see his family again.

Ricardo had planned to stay in Cepeda only two weeks before reentering the United States. When he saw Felipe, however, he knew he couldn't leave that soon.

"He's so thin," he said to his mother. "And so pale."

"I know," his mother replied. "The doctor says there is little hope that he will live. There is a terrible illness in his blood."

A month later, Felipe died. Ricardo had several friends who had lost a young brother or a sister. Now, he himself knew the pain that such a death can cause. Mixed with the pain, though, there was gratitude that he had been able to see Felipe before he died and that he could be there to comfort his mother and his sister.

Ricardo's second entry into the United States was much easier than the first. After taking a bus to the border, he was able to pay a *coyote* to take him across the river in a boat, then he rode to San Antonio in a van driven by another *coyote*. The day after his arrival, he applied for a dishwasher's job in the same restaurant where he'd worked

THE UNCERTAIN JOURNEY

before his deportation. While he waited for an opening, he did yard work and hauling with Pedro, who had bought an old truck while Ricardo was in Mexico.

Less than a month passed before Ricardo was called back to work by the restaurant owner. It was then that he and Ana got married and found an apartment of their own. In more ways than one, the marriage marked a turning point in Ricardo's life. Ana had been born in the United States and spoke fluent English, and she insisted that Ricardo learn more than the common English words and phrases she had taught him during their courtship. After their marriage, she demanded that they speak only English in their home.

At times, this rule angered Ricardo, and he refused to speak at all. Later, however, when there was an opening for a cook at the restaurant, he was offered that job because he was able to speak both English and Spanish. He now had a job that paid six dollars an hour, better wages than he'd ever dreamed of making. Besides sending money home, he even dared to open a savings account in a bank. His goal was to save enough to buy another truck and become a full partner in Pedro's gardening and hauling business. That plan suffered a setback when Pedro was deported and never returned to San Antonio.

For six years, Ricardo worked at the restaurant, and Ana worked as a teacher's aide. When the federal amnesty program was put into effect, Ricardo qualified because he had been a continuous resident of the United States since 1981. After filing his amnesty application, Ricardo received permission to live and

––––––– *The Eyes and Ears of La Migra . . .* –––––––

to work in this country. At last, he need have no fear of crossing the border to visit his family. He need not fear the visits of the immigration authorities. And he could start progressing toward his goal—that of owning his own business.

Now, Ricardo has reached that goal—he owns a catering truck that provides lunches and snacks to workers in office buildings and construction sites. Ana makes all the tacos and enchiladas and burritos, which are so delicious that no matter how many are loaded onto the truck, there are none left when Ricardo returns late in the afternoon.

Ana and Ricardo now have a one-year-old son and are planning a monthlong visit to Cepeda. Ricardo hopes to bring his mother and sister into the United States on visitors' passes. Once here, he is determined that they will stay.

2

Adios, Mi Niños

Alicia was twenty-eight years old and the mother of four small children when her husband was killed in a factory accident in La Libertad, El Salvador. For several months, she tried to support her family by taking in laundry and by sewing, but the average of five dollars a week that she made wasn't enough to keep food in their one-room house.

When her brother, Maximo, returned from the United States to La Libertad, he told Alicia of the money she could make as a maid in that wealthy country to the north. Within a week, she had decided to travel with Maximo when he returned to *El Norte*. The decision was an extremely difficult one. She had never spent so much as one day away from her children. Now, she could be separated from them for months, even years. Even though her mother was able to care for them, the thought of not being with them was almost too much to bear.

But what choice did she have? If she remained in El

Salvador, she would never have enough money to feed her family properly. If one of them became ill, she would not be able to buy medicine. Two of her own brothers had died when they were infants. There was hardly a family in La Libertad that had not lost a child to malnutrition or disease.

On the other hand, if she went to *El Norte* and found a high-paying job, the money she sent home would enable her children to grow plump and strong. And next year, her eldest would have shoes and proper clothing so he could attend school.

Alicia's last day in El Salvador was spent as if it were any other day. She rose early, prepared the corn for breakfast and the beans for dinner, then walked to the other end of town to collect the dirty clothing and linens from the homes of the town officials. For hours, she carried water from the well, heated it over an open fire, then scrubbed, rinsed, and wrung sheets, shirts, and trousers, all the while keeping a vigilant eye on her children as they played in the dirt of the small yard. The sun was starting to sink when she folded the laundry and carried it back across town.

As she fed her family that evening, she was painfully aware that this was the last meal she would prepare for them for a long time. A short while later, just before the youngsters lay down on the mattress on the floor, Alicia told her four-year-old daughter and her five-year-old son that she would be leaving before they awoke the next morning.

"But for how long?" asked her son.

─────── THE UNCERTAIN JOURNEY ───────

"That I do not know," Alicia said. "But be assured that I will return as soon as I can. Meanwhile, your grandmother will care for you."

Her answer seemed to satisfy the children. Soon, they were asleep.

The next morning, an hour before the sun rose, Alicia stuffed a change of clothing and some bread and cheese into a canvas bag, then sewed three hundred dollars into the waistband of her jeans. The money had been loaned to her by one of her laundry customers, who had accepted her house as collateral.

By the time her mother arose from her small cot in the corner of the room, Alicia was ready to leave. There were tears in the eyes of both women as they said good-bye and as Alicia took a long last look at her sleeping youngsters. *"Adios, mi niños,"* she said, pulling the thin blanket up over their shoulders. Then she walked out the door and began the two-mile walk to the bus station where Maximo was to meet her.

The bus trip from La Libertad to San Salvador took only an hour; the one from San Salvador to the northern border town of Tecun Unam in Guatemala took less than a day. Maximo and Alicia were surrounded by *coyotes* as soon as they arrived in Tecun Unam. Maximo chose a young man who, for fifty dollars, said he could lead them over the Suchiate River into Ciudad Hidalgo in Mexico. The price included the bribe that had to be paid to the Guatemalan officials at the bus terminal. For five dollars each, they would ask no questions of the travelers.

Later that evening, the *coyote* led his group of *pollos* to the river that ran along the border between Mexico and Guatemala. Barefoot, holding each other's hands, keeping a sharp eye out for bandits who would rob and perhaps beat them, Maximo and Alicia waded through the chest-high water to the opposite bank. In Ciudad Hidalgo, their *coyote* left them after their arrival at a "safe house," which was owned by a Mexican woman. Alicia had never seen such a house—not even the officials in La Libertad lived in such large rooms filled with such sturdy furniture.

The next morning, the *pollos* were given a breakfast of bacon, eggs, and toast. Alicia had never tasted bacon before, and the few eggs she had been able to buy she had given to her children.

Maximo grinned when he saw how impressed she was by her surroundings. "Many *Americanos* live in houses such as this and have meals such as this," he said. "And they hire women such as you to do the cooking and the cleaning and to care for their children. They pay good wages and also provide a room, sometimes with a television set in it."

A television set! Alicia's laundry customers had such things, but Alicia herself had never seen one up close.

After breakfast, Alicia gave the woman *coyote* thirty-five dollars to get them on the highway that would take them north to Tapachula and for a map that showed them how to proceed from there. The *coyote* told Alicia to change from her ragged blue jeans and old sandals into the skirt and blouse and the leather dress shoes she had brought with her. "And you should leave your other belongings with me," she said. "If you carry a bundle, you might as well wear a big sign marked SIN PAPELES. You probably wouldn't get past the first checkpoint."

Although Alicia and Maximo would be left with only the clothing on their backs and their packets of money, they followed the woman's advice. After all, Alicia thought, with all the money I'm going to make, I can buy myself a new dress and still have money left to send to my mother.

The group of *pollos* crowded into a station wagon, then, using only back roads, the *coyote* took them to the highway and waited with them until a rickety bus came along. "Pray that you don't get stopped at the Manguito checkpoint up the road," she said. "After you pass Tapachula, you can get off the bus before the next checkpoint, then walk to town and take a train to Arriago."

She also told them not to talk too much in public. "You may look like Mexicans," she said, "but the sound of your voices will identify you as Central Americans."

It wasn't long before Alicia had reason to be grateful for the *coyote*'s advice. At Manguito, a Mexican immigration official waved the bus down, boarded it, then walked down the aisle, glancing at each passenger. When he left the vehicle, he took two women with him. Both of them wore jeans and tennis shoes, carried a suitcase, and talked in the high-pitched voices that are common to Central Americans.

It was while they were waiting for the train to Arriago

Adios, Mi Niños

that a family of Guatemalans, a husband and wife and their two teenaged daughters, struck up a conversation with Maximo and Alicia. When the group arrived in Arriago, they decided to save money by sharing the same hotel room. When Maximo took $20 from his wallet to pay his and Alicia's share, the wife grabbed it, paid for the room, and pocketed the change. "We are broke," she said. "We will pay our share later."

Alicia saw the anger in Maximo's eyes, but she knew he didn't dare get into a fight. It was better to be cheated by these people than to end up in a Mexican jail. Later, when she and her brother had a few moments alone, they agreed that the sooner they broke away from their traveling companions, the better off they would be. Although both of them were exhausted, neither slept well that night. They were afraid that they would wake to find that they had been robbed. Before the sun rose, Maximo and Alicia crept from the room, then climbed into a boxcar that was part of a train headed for the state of Oaxaca. A moment later, a railroad employee appeared in the open door of the car.

"Fifty dollars will buy my silence, both now and at the Ixtepec checkpoint," he said.

The payment of the bribe would take half of the money that Alicia and Maximo had left, but they had to pay it or end up in jail waiting many weeks to be deported back to El Salvador.

During the next month, the travelers inched their way toward the northern border, boarding various buses, getting off them before each checkpoint, then walking along dusty back roads until it was safe to board another bus.

THE UNCERTAIN JOURNEY

Finally they arrived at Ciudad Juarez, which is divided from the Texas city of El Paso by only a shallow river. For all practical purposes, the two cities are one, with men and women crossing over to work in the United States during the day, then returning to Juarez at night to live in the shacks that form the *colonias,* the small poverty-stricken settlements that exist along both sides of the river.

Maximo and Alicia spent the night on the Mexican side of the river, then crossed to the American side the next morning. Alicia thought their journey was over, and she was shocked to see that here in the United States, there were men and women wearing tattered clothing; there were children with no shoes and with stringy hair and smudged faces and the shadow of hunger in their eyes. They reminded Alicia of her own children, and her heart ached.

"Is this *El Norte*?" she asked Maximo. "Where are the grand houses? Where are the rich people?"

Maximo laughed and led her down the dusty street. "Wait," he replied. When they reached a telephone booth, he made a long-distance call to some friends in Albuquerque, New Mexico.

"My sister and I, we're in El Paso," he said. "We have no money for bus fare. Can you help us?"

Two minutes later, Maximo hung up the telephone. "They're going to send us some money by the telegraph. By the end of the week, we'll be in in Albuquerque."

Alicia hoped he was right. She was hungry. She was tired. But most of all, she was worried about her family.

Adios, Mi Niños

By now, they would be running low on the beans and corn meal she'd left them. Without money, they would soon be starving.

Maximo and Alicia arrived in Albuquerque three days later. By nightfall, they had joined Maximo's friends in their hotel room on the outskirts of the city. The three men and two women living there welcomed the newcomers. The next day, one of the women took Alicia to an employment agency that found jobs for illegals who wanted to work as domestics. She was told the only work available at that time was in a motel or a laundry. There was nothing that came with a room containing a soft bed and a television set, but Alicia was glad that there were any jobs at all. She made an immediate decision.

"The laundry," she said. "That's what I did in El Salvador." She was hired the following day, and by the end of the week, Maximo had found a job at a carwash. Maximo said he would pay their share of the rent for the hotel room, so Alicia would be able to send most of her pay to her mother. Two weeks later, Alicia mailed a $150 money order to El Salvador. That was a fortune—more than enough to make a payment on the loan and to buy food for the family.

The temperature in the large steamy building where Alicia worked often rose to above ninety degrees, and lifting the heavy bundles of damp linens made her back ache. Still, the work was no harder than the work she had done in La Libertad, and she was making three dollars an hour, a fortune compared to what she had been making. Every

THE UNCERTAIN JOURNEY

day, she worked faster and harder so her *patron,* her boss, would be pleased with her.

But one day, just four months after she had started her job, one of the workers spotted an official car parked near the main door of the building, and the whisper of ¡*Migra! Migra!* sped up one aisle of the building and down the next. As Alicia followed the other illegal workers who were hurrying toward the back door of the building, she remembered what Maximo had said: "Keep your money with you always. That way, if you get caught by the immigration, you'll have the means of getting back to Albuquerque. And never tell *la migra* that you're from El Salvador. Say, instead, that you're from Mexico. That way, they'll probably just put you on a bus and drop you off on the other side of the Mexican border. From there, it's easy to cross back over."

Alicia was one of twenty-five workers who were caught in the parking lot behind the laundry building. By the next afternoon, she was getting off a bus in El Paso and being directed toward the southern bank of the river by members of the border patrol. The following morning, Thursday, she returned to El Paso by simply walking over a bridge with several other women. Within an hour, she was on a bus that was bound for Albuquerque. By Monday, she was back at work in the laundry, resentful that *la migra* had caused her to lose almost a week's wages. Somehow, she must find a way to make that up—the more money she earned, the faster she could return to La Libertad and to her family. There was scarcely a moment when her mind was not filled with thoughts of her children. Do they miss me?

she wondered. Are they in good health? Do they understand why I had to leave them?

During the two years that Alicia has spent in the United States, she has been able to elude the "sweeps" that the Immigration and Naturalization Service periodically stages in the businesses that hire undocumented workers. She has already reached one of her goals—that of paying off the loan on her home.

When Alicia returns home, she will probably be traveling with Manuel, a Salvadoran friend of her brother's. Alicia and Manuel plan to be married, but she wants to wait until her family can be present at the ceremony. In two more years, with both of them saving money, they will be able to add two rooms to Alicia's house and to buy equipment for a woodworking shop for Manuel.

As long as they stay in the United States, both Manuel and Alicia will be subject to seizure by the immigration authorities. One of their big worries is that one of them will be picked up, leaving the other one behind. Meanwhile, both of them go to work every day, pick up extra odd jobs whenever they can, and remain constantly alert and prepared to run and hide.

"El Norte *has been good to me," says Alicia. "But I live only for the day when I can see my children again."*

3

No Problema

Jorge's home is in a southern Mexican village that is nothing more than a collection of little houses built of adobe or cinder blocks. There are no trees lining the bumpy dirt road that meanders through town. A few scrawny dogs and an occasional chicken or turkey scratch in the dust, and children in ragged clothing play with sticks and an old rubber ball. The women watch over the children, haul water from the well, and make the meals. The men walk to the nearby towns to look for work. The fact that there is seldom any work to be found does not keep them from returning day after day. They believe that, in large measure, fate has already laid out the paths of their lives and they face obstacles and mishaps with a quiet self-assurance. But they still stand ready to seize any opportunity. If, on a certain day, their fate decrees that they should build a wall or dig a ditch or load a truck, they want to be available.

On Jorge's sixteenth birthday, he decided that it was his

No Problema

fate to go the United States. There, he might find a good steady job and send money home to help his parents support his three younger brothers. Without his help, it was likely that none of them would be able to finish primary school. Following the advice of older men who had crossed the border and returned several times, Jorge made his way to Arizona, where he became a picker in the orchards around Phoenix.

But then came December, and because of the seasonal rains, the *braceros* were working only five days a week, and at Christmas, they were forced to take a seven-day break. According to the experienced pickers, it was time to go to Florida, where the citrus season lasted well into the summer. Jorge and nine of his fellow workers pooled their money and, for three hundred dollars, bought a twenty-year-old station wagon. On a cold rainy afternoon, they started their cross-country journey. The driver was Emilio, a gray-haired "superpicker" who had traveled the route so often he had memorized not only all of the interstate highways but also the back roads that were necessary to avoid the immigration officers.

Emilio was to share the driving with Inocencio, the only other member of the group who had a driver's license.

The two drivers sat in the front, the rest climbed into the back. With the blankets and knapsacks, there was not even an inch to spare. Jorge considered himself lucky to be sitting by a window. At least he would have someone's elbow crushing his ribs on only one side of his body. With a lurch and a grinding of gears, they were moving, and Jorge forgot his discomfort in the anticipation of going to a place where there was work for everyone, seven days a week, twelve to fifteen hours a day.

The men had been on the road only a short time when it became evident that their overloaded vehicle had several problems. Its automatic transmission kept slipping out of gear, its thin tires had little traction on the wet roads, and at speeds over fifty miles an hour, it swayed so badly that the steering was almost impossible to control.

As he struggled to keep the station wagon on the right side of the road, Emilio laughed. *"No problema.* What did we expect for only three hundred dollars? It's a good car. It will get us to Florida."

As gusts of wind buffeted the station wagon, the driver went slower and slower. At first, the men chatted and laughed at each other's jokes. Then, when the weather grew colder, they found that the heater warmed only Emilio and Inocencio. The men in back had to burrow under blankets and jackets. When the sun went down, the road curved up into the pine forests of the snow-covered mountains and the cold caused Jorge's hands and feet to become numb.

At Flagstaff, the driver stopped to refuel the station wagon and to put fluid into the transmission. Reluctant to release any of the body heat that had accumulated around them, the rest of the passengers didn't move. Jorge was used to being hungry so he could ignore the emptiness in his stomach. But the cold had crept deep into his bones, and he longed for the constant sunshine of his native land. Still, despite his discomfort, he was grateful to be with good friends and to be in *El Norte* and on his way to

― No Problema ―

Florida, where there would be plenty of work for everyone.

Ten minutes later, the travelers were back on the icy road. Then, on a steep switchback, the vehicle went into a skid, and the driver turned the wrong way to pull out of it. When the back of the wagon fishtailed, Jorge sat straight up, prepared for a crash, his heart pounding. *"Madre mia,"* he murmured as the back of the wagon plowed into a snowbank along the side of the road. There was a crunching sound when it made contact with a railing.

Jorge tossed aside his covering and, along with the other passengers, climbed out to push the wagon back onto the road. When they surveyed the damage, they found that the left taillight was smashed and the bumper had been pushed into the crumpled rear fender. But *no problema,* everyone agreed. The car could still run. Fate was smiling upon them.

Emilio had been driving slowly before the accident. Now, Inocencio took the wheel and drove so slowly that it took twelve hours instead of the usual six to get from Flagstaff to Albuquerque, New Mexico. Jorge wasn't bothered by their snaillike progress. After all, as long as they were heading in the right direction, there was no need for undue haste. What did bother him was that so much of the distance was being traveled with their headlights burrowing through snow flurries and wind blowing in gusts strong enough that it threatened to blow them off the road.

It was still snowing when they reached the Texas border. As they drove into Amarillo, they found themselves

THE UNCERTAIN JOURNEY

in the middle of the late afternoon rush-hour traffic. It was at this time that the window defroster stopped working. Every ten minutes they had to stop, get out of the car, and using their fingernails and the edges of their wallets, scrape the layer of ice off the front and rear windows. By now the storm had become a blizzard. "It's no use going on," Inocencio said. "The roads are too slippery, and I can't see where I'm going."

"Better to get to Florida late than not at all," Emilio said. The other passengers nodded their assent. After all, what difference would a few more hours make? The orchards would still be there, wouldn't they?

After driving to a motel, Inocencio chose Jorge to go into the office and rent a room. "Just tell the clerk you and your father need a place to stay," he said. "He'll believe a young boy like you."

Jorge didn't like telling a lie, but he knew how important it was for everyone to save as much money as possible. A few minutes later, he came out of the office waving a key. Good fortune had not deserted the group of *sin papeles*. Because of the storm, the clerk hadn't wanted to leave the comfort of the office to see how many tenants would actually be sharing the room.

The travelers forgot their hunger as soon as the warmth of the room enveloped them. Sprawled across the two twin beds, spread out on the carpeted floor, curled up in a corner, they were all asleep within minutes. Jorge slept for seven hours, until he was awakened by a touch on his shoulder.

* * *

No Problema

Early the next morning, the group was back on the road. The weather had improved, and after a breakfast of hamburgers and french fries, so had the spirits of the travelers. They sang ranchero songs:

There comes a large cloud of dust with no consideration.
Women, children, and old men are being driven to the border.
Good-bye, beloved countrymen, we are being deported,
But we are not outlaws, we come to work.

If they throw one out through Laredo, ten will come in through Mexicali.
If another is kicked out through Tijuana, six will come in through Nogales.

Then they started exchanging stories about some of their experiences as *sin papeles*. Jorge listened closely, as Emilio, who was forty and had been in the United States for many years, told of how he had once crossed the border.

"Three friends and I, we climbed into the tank of a cement mixer. When the driver approached the border, he turned the mixer on. *Ay, ay, ay.* We were tossed about and got bruises everywhere, but the border patrol suspected nothing." He laughed at the memory. "And other times I crossed by hiding in the hood of a car and underneath the car."

Another man told of his experience in "riding the rails."

"To get from here to there, I often hop the freight trains," he said. "I find a boxcar and ride on top of the axles or on the air tank underneath a flat car. Sometimes

THE UNCERTAIN JOURNEY

sparks fly out, but when they land on me, they go out right away."

"Never run beneath the cars," said another older man. "If they start up, you could get cut in half."

"I once saw a man get run over by the wheels," said Emilio. He paused for a moment. "I stayed beside him as he died."

Later that day, the heater stopped working entirely and so did the windshield wipers. Emilio tinkered with some of the wiring under the hood, but had no success. They were forced to stop at a gas station to have a mechanic try to solve the problems.

"Look at this battery," the mechanic said. "It's too small for a station wagon."

Jorge joined Emilio as he looked down into the engine. Sure enough, the battery was so small that if it hadn't been held in place by the battery cables, it would have bounced out.

"That's why the heater isn't working," the mechanic continued. "Not enough power."

The price he quoted for a battery with the trade-in was a fair one, as was what he charged for fixing the windshield wipers. The group was lucky to have happened upon an honest mechanic. Many others, seeing a group of poor Mexicans, would have charged much more than the job was worth.

The state of Oklahoma favored the travelers with fairly good weather until they approached Tulsa. Here, rain and sleet made the highway slippery, and Inocencio had to take

No Problema

care to avoid the tractor-trailer rigs that were sliding in and out of the lanes. Two of them had gone off the road and were resting in a gully. Then, as the station wagon crept around a curve, its windshield wipers barely keeping up with the pelting rain, a large moving van loomed up directly in front of it.

"Stop, stop," yelled Emilio.

But his cry came too late. The squeal of tires was followed by a jolt and a crashing sound that caused everyone in the station wagon to sit up. Jorge groaned when he saw that they had rear-ended the stalled van. *"Ay, ay, ay,* we're in trouble now," he said. The van's driver would no doubt call the police, the police would put them in jail and call *la migra*. Within a few seconds, their chance to make good money in Florida had vanished.

Before Inocencio had a chance to get out of the car, a bulky truck driver was standing on the passenger side tapping on the window. Emilio rolled it down. "Sorry," he said. "We'll pay for—"

"Hey, it was my fault," the truck driver said. "I should have pulled off onto the shoulder as soon as my engine stalled. You guys all right?"

"Sure, no problem," Emilio said.

"Back up," said the driver. "Let's see what the damage is."

Both headlights were smashed, the bumper rested on top of the crumpled hood, the fenders were bent, and the door on the passenger side could no longer be opened. "Hey, it still runs," said Inocencio. "Everything is okay."

THE UNCERTAIN JOURNEY

He was anxious to get started again. The longer they stayed there, the better the chance that a policeman would drive by and stop to see what had happened.

"Well, you'll have to get those headlights fixed." The truck driver pulled out his wallet and handed them forty dollars. "This ought to cover it."

"Thank you, friend," said Emilio. He and Inocencio got back into the car as the driver walked away. Again, good fortune had been riding with them. In one day, they had met two honest men.

To avoid paying a mechanic, Emilio went to an auto parts store and bought two headlights. After removing the old lights and taping the new ones securely in place, he grinned. "Now we have an extra twenty dollars." To celebrate, they bought a bucket of chicken from *el viejito,* the little old man, Colonel Sanders.

As they continued their journey, their stomachs full, luxuriating in the warmth from a fully functioning heater, everyone except the driver dozed. They woke to see green trees instead of the barren landscape of a Midwest winter. At the dawning of their fourth day on the road, they crossed over the Mississippi River into Arkansas.

All the way across Arkansas and into Tennessee, the weather was warm and the station wagon continued to run. Then, just as they left Knoxville to head south, there was a loud noise and the wagon swerved, just missing a car in the neighboring lane. Wrestling the steering wheel, Emilio bumped to a stop on the shoulder. "It's a blow out," he said. "Who will go back to town to get another tire?"

No Problema

Jorge welcomed the chance to exercise his cramped muscles. "I'll go," he said. An hour later, he returned with a retread. After a quick tire change, they were back on the interstate, headed toward Georgia. At Macon, they left the main highway to avoid being spotted by immigration officials. At this time of the year, with so many pickers entering Florida, *la migra* would be everywhere.

The sun was setting when the travelers reached central Florida. They passed woods and lakes and fields of tomatoes, melons, strawberries, and sugarcane. And there were the citrus groves—vast forests of trees laden with oranges, lemons, and grapefruit. By tomorrow, they would be joining all the other *braceros,* the farm workers who had come to this place, lured by the thought of the dollars they could earn. Life is good, thought Jorge.

Emilio parked the station wagon in a remote corner of an orchard, then got out, stretched, and patted the vehicle on one of its crumpled fenders. "What a friend you are," he said. "You brought us to the work."

But that night, there was no more thought of work. The men had a meal of oranges picked from the trees. And then they spread their blankets on the ground and slept under the stars until the rays of the Florida sun awakened them.

When the picking season ended in Florida, Jorge started working his way around the country, following the ripening crops. In Arkansas, he picked cotton, in Texas, grapefruit, in Michigan, apples and cucumbers. He went to New York to pick onions and strawberries, then worked his way along the Canadian border to Washington to harvest asparagus, and to California to pick lettuce, peaches, and olives.

At times, he made three hundred dollars a day, but then it would rain for two days or a sudden cold front would freeze the crop, and he would make nothing. Once, the car in which he was riding broke down and he arrived in Michigan three days late to find that all the jobs were taken. He had to travel several hundred miles before he found more work. Other changes in plans were triggered by news of unusually good or bad weather, of a bumper crop or a crop failure, or of an early or late crop. Jorge was grateful for the times when he found work. When there was a setback, he traveled on from farm to farm, always certain that fate would lead him to another job, another opportunity to earn the money his family needed.

There were times when the cry of *¡Migra! Migra!* sounded the alarm, and he and his fellow workers ran from their encampments into the orchards and scattered in all directions. Those who weren't caught usually crept back within a few hours and went back to work the next day. Jorge was one of the truly fortunate ones: He always managed to elude his pursuers. And every month, his family received part of what he earned, sometimes more, sometimes less, but always something.

Jorge has been following the crops for almost five years. He is happy that he is able to earn a living, but he is tired of traveling and of hiding from the immigration officials. Within the next few months, he will return home for a visit. By that time, one of his

No Problema

brothers will be out of school and will be able to help support his family.

Jorge's current dream is to own his own farm in Mexico. With his brother helping to shoulder the burden he has been carrying, he believes it is his fate to have that dream come true.

"Three or maybe four more years in the United States," he says. "That will give me enough money to buy some good land and a tractor and a cow. In Mexico, that is wealth."

(LEFT) Stationed at a busy intersection from dawn to dusk, this undocumented worker sells peanuts and oranges. Photo by Gary McCarthy.

(BELOW) Most confrontations between illegal aliens and border patrol officers are nonviolent. Courtesy of U.S. Immigration and Naturalization Service.

After being escorted back to Mexico by U.S. Border Patrol officers, this worker will probably wait awhile, then cross back into the United States at another point. Photo by Gary McCarthy.

(TOP) Perhaps these twenty-eight foreign workers were lucky to be caught. Crammed into a small truck with no ventilation or water, some of them could have died before they reached their destination. Courtesy of U.S. Immigration and Naturalization Service.

(BOTTOM) These workers are waiting for the sun to go down so they can cross la frontera, *the border between Mexico and the United States.* Photo by Gary McCarthy.

Radio communication enables one border patrolman to notify another of a sighting of a group of illegal border crossers. Courtesy of U.S. Immigration and Naturalization Service.

To sell his flowers, a peddler takes his chances with traffic. Photo by Gary McCarthy.

Ricardo. Photo by Robert Poynter.

Francisco. Photo by Robert Poynter.

Arnulfo. Photo by Robert Poynter.

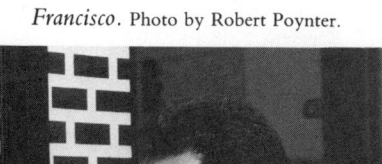

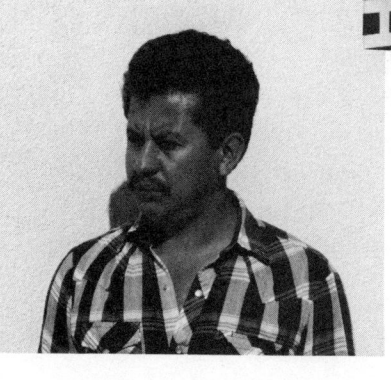

Primo. Photo by Robert Poynter.

4

How Long Is a Row?

Jose's last job had ended three weeks earlier. Since then, he had spent his days walking from farm to farm asking everyone he met if there was something he could do to earn a few dollars. Finally, when a farmer said he needed someone to plant onions, Jose jumped at the chance.

"I'll pay you two dollars a row," the farmer said.

The wage he offered sounded fair enough, and Jose was anxious to get started. He and his wife, Lupe, and their three children had eaten nothing but a few slices of bread for the last two days.

The farmer led Jose to a large shed and showed him how to cut the onions to prepare them for planting. Jose soon had two boxes filled with cut onions. Thinking such an amount would be more than enough for a row, he picked up the boxes and walked toward the door of the shed.

"Fill up some more boxes," the farmer said. "That way, you'll be able to finish a row before you come back."

"Just how long is a row?" Jose asked.

―――――― *How Long Is a Row?* ――――――

"Long enough," the farmer said. "Just keep cutting."

The rows must be long indeed, Jose thought. All that work for only two dollars.

Jose spent the next fifteen days bending from the waist to plant the cut onions in the muddy field. For each day's work, he received only eight dollars. Once again, an employer had taken advantage of the fact that he was an undocumented worker who was desperate for a job.

Jose,␣Lupe, and their three children are from Ecuador. When his parents died, he inherited their three-room house, and he also owned a small fishing boat. Even with these advantages, he was able to eke out only a marginal living for his family.

Jose's fortunes worsened with the arrival of *El Niño*. This weather phenomenon, which occurs every ten or fifteen years, is caused by a change in the ocean currents. The change causes the water temperature to rise, and the fish in the area swim northward in search of cooler water. For almost two years, Jose's nets had come up almost empty. At times, it was only through the generosity of Lupe's parents that his children were fed. But Jose knew that he couldn't depend on that generosity much longer. His father-in-law was very ill and had had to give up his job in the sugar mill where he had worked most of his life. The little money they had saved would soon be gone.

Jose worried about what would happen if the fish continued to stay away. For the first time, he began to consider traveling to the *Estados Unidos* (the United States), as two of his uncles had done five years earlier. In every letter, they told of the high wages they were making.

THE UNCERTAIN JOURNEY

One morning, Jose left his fishing nets spread on the beach and traveled to Quayaquil to seek information about how he could travel to this land where everyone always had money in his pocket. Within minutes of his arrival at the bus station in Quayaquil, he was approached by a stocky man who was smoking a big cigar.

"Are you interested in traveling north?" the man asked.

Jose nodded. "Yes."

"Have you made any arrangements?" the man asked.

"No."

"I can help you." The man led Jose to a small restaurant nearby. "Coffee for me and my friend," he said to the waitress.

During the next thirty minutes, Jose found that the *coyote's* price to transport Jose and his family to California would be three thousand dollars; that there was work there for not only him but also his wife and even his two older children, who were twelve and fourteen years old; and that their food and shelter would be provided by their employer.

"I have a contract with a farmer in California," the *coyote* said. "One month from now, his crops will be ready for harvest, and he is depending on me to bring him workers."

"Three thousand dollars—that's a lot of money," Jose said. "When will you be leaving?"

"Two weeks from now—on Thursday."

"I will try to be here," Jose replied.

The *coyote* smiled. "If not you, there will be many others."

How Long Is a Row?

Later, as Jose waited for a bus to return to his village, he saw the *coyote* approach another shabbily dressed man. "Where are you going?" he asked. Soon, the two were walking down the street toward the coffee shop.

Two weeks wasn't enough time to sell a house and a boat and to ask for and receive money from Jose's uncles in the United States. Almost two months passed before Jose and his family arrived in Quayaquil with their clothing crammed into cloth bags and their money folded into a packet that had been sewed inside the waistband of Jose's trousers.

As his wife and children ate some of the boiled sweet potatoes they brought with them, Jose walked through the bus station. He looked into every face, knowing there must be some *coyotes* here, hoping that one of them would approach him. It had happened so quickly the first time. Now he had the money, but would he find someone who was willing to do business with him?

Finally, after an hour had passed, a thin man walked past Jose, then turned and spoke to him. "Would you like to travel north?" the man asked.

"Yes," Jose replied. "Also my wife and three children."

The man thought for a moment. "Four thousand dollars," he said.

"I can pay only three."

"I know where there is work for you," the man replied. "Give me the three when we board the plane, and you can pay the rest later."

The next morning, as the sun was rising, Jose and his family joined six of his fellow Ecuadorans in the small

THE UNCERTAIN JOURNEY

aircraft that was to carry them to the United States. Early the following day, the plane landed in a remote airfield in a desert area of central California. The trip had been a bumpy one, and the coughing and sputtering of the plane's engine had made Jose nervous. As they walked toward the edge of the airfield, where a battered van was waiting for them, he was grateful for the feel of the earth under his feet.

The group of *sin papeles* climbed into the back of the van. When they were all seated, the driver gave them a warning. "*La migra* is watching the roads. For your own safety, I must lock you in." He slammed the door. A few moments later, the van started to move. Jose smiled at Lupe and ruffled the hair of his eldest child. Things were going well. By tomorrow they would be working in the fields, earning the money that would buy them a better life than they had ever known.

For over two hours, the *sin papeles* rode in the back of the van. Jose grew drowsy from lack of air, and as the time passed, the heat became oppressive. Lupe was trying to quiet the baby, whose fretful whimperings had become shrill cries. One of the passengers, a thin gray-haired man, banged on the front of the compartment, trying to get the driver's attention.

"Stop!" he cried. "Let us out! We need air!"

But there was no response. Jose felt a moment of panic. Had they come so far just to die of suffocation?

Finally, just when Jose felt he would not be able to take another breath, the van stopped. A moment later, he heard

How Long Is a Row?

the scraping of a key in the lock, then the doors swung open. "Here we are," the driver said.

The van was parked in a grove of trees near a large barn, from which a broad-shouldered bearded man emerged. Nearby, there was a tractor attached to a small flat trailer that was piled high with ladders. A few minutes later, the driver drove away in the van.

"You and the kids go on into the barn. We'll try to find some work for you later." The bearded man spoke in Spanish and pointed to Lupe. "The rest of you get on the trailer. Hurry now. There's fruit waiting to be picked."

Jose and the other workers climbed onto the trailer and sat on top of the ladders. The bearded man, whose name was Hugo, started the engine of the tractor and, with a great jerk, the trailer began moving at high speed along the rutted road that led to the orchard. To keep from being bounced off, Jose clung to a ladder while another worker clung to him. The tractor kicked up clouds of dust that filled everyone's eyes, and with each back-breaking bump and jolt, Jose prayed that he would end this journey with no broken bones.

Ten minutes later, when the tractor came to an abrupt stop, Jose felt he must be bruised from head to toe. He slid from the trailer onto the ground and stood there bewildered while Hugo pointed toward the trees that stood on the other side of an irrigation ditch. At the signal, each worker pulled a ladder from the trailer, mounted it on his shoulder, and stooped to pick a burlap bag from a pile that lay on the ground. Jose followed their lead, ending up with the last ladder, a rickety affair with loose rungs.

THE UNCERTAIN JOURNEY

By now, the other more experienced pickers had jumped the irrigation ditch; each had chosen a tree that was fully laden with fruit and positioned his ladder against it. "Hurry! Hurry!" Hugo shouted to Jose, who quickly jumped the ditch. As he landed on the other side, one end of the ladder nose-dived into the soft dirt, abruptly stopping his forward motion and pushing the other end into his shoulder. The painful blow caused him to pause for a moment. "I told you to hurry!" Hugo yelled.

A skilled picker handles his heavy twenty-foot ladder as if it were made of balsa wood. He knows exactly how to position it so it will remain steady as he reaches for the furthest branches. He can balance himself without hanging onto either the ladder or a branch, because by using both hands, he gets the job done twice as fast, thus earning twice as much money.

Jose had never picked fruit before, so he had much to learn during his first few hours on the job. And while he was learning, Hugo grew more and more impatient and abusive. Each time Jose dumped a bag into the wooden collecting crates, Hugo complained that the bag hadn't been filled to the top, that the fruit had brown sun spots, or was too small or too big, or was bumpy with a superthick rind. Twice he picked out the offending fruit and threw it at Jose. Then he reprimanded him for stopping to wipe some dirt and perspiration from his face and for overlooking an orange hidden on a high branch. "Lazy bum!" he yelled. "You should go back to where you came from!"

Toward the end of the day, Jose's work had improved and Hugo had fewer complaints. But just before quitting time, Jose's foot slipped as he stepped onto a rung of his ladder. Down he fell with fifty pounds of oranges in the bag around his neck, landing with a thud at the foot of the tree. Dazed, he looked up to see Hugo staring down at him. "You are not only lazy," Hugo snarled. "You are also clumsy."

If I'm lucky, Jose thought, I will only be fired. If I'm unlucky, I will be reported to *la migra*. He said nothing to Hugo, just rose, collected the oranges that had spilled from his bag, and climbed back up the ladder to pick the last of the fruit from the tree.

Neither of Jose's fears became reality: he was neither fired nor picked up by immigration officials. Taking advantage of the lessons he learned during that first long, painful day, within a week, he was keeping up with many of the other workers, although still far behind the "superpickers," whose hands moved so fast they appeared as a blur and who were able to make thirty dollars a day while Jose was making ten or fifteen.

Each evening as the sun went down, Jose and the other pickers were taken to a row of dirty, unpainted one-room sheds where they spent the night. Jose and his family had to share their small space with two other men. The workers bought their groceries from Hugo, who charged them twice as much as they would have paid in a store. Their meals were cooked out-of-doors over an open fire.

The job in the orchard lasted for a month, then Jose and his family went to another farm, where everyone except the youngest child picked tomatoes. Here, on cold nights, they were allowed to sleep in the barn. When the weather was warm, they spread sheets of plastic on the ground and slept outside in a sheltered grove of trees.

Picking oranges and tomatoes was not easy work, but Jose and Lupe soon found that picking lemons was even harder. The filled bags weighed eighty pounds, almost enough to pull a woman or a small man off the ladder. The pickers had to watch out for inch-long thorns shaped like pencil ends, and the lemons couldn't be pulled from the branch—they had to be clipped with a special tool. Even when gloves were worn, this instrument caused sharp pains in the tender muscle of the palm of the hand. By the end of the day, the pickers' hands hurt so much they had to use only their fingertips. Their shoulder muscles ached, and sore neck muscles prevented them from moving their heads from side to side.

Life in *El Norte* certainly wasn't easy, but Jose and Lupe had money in their pockets, and their stomachs were full. They would not have had it so good in their homeland.

When winter arrived, and there was frost on the ground in the morning, farm work became hard to find.

"We'll go to Los Angeles," Jose said. "There, we can rent a room, so the children will be warm at night. In such a big city, there must be work for us." That afternoon, they boarded a southward-bound bus. Upon their arrival in Los Angeles, they rented a two-room apartment, and with the remainder of the money they had saved, bought a ten-pound sack of beans and twenty pounds of potatoes.

How Long Is a Row?

Before that stock of food ran out, at least one of them would have to earn some more money.

Lupe was the first to find a job: She went to work sewing blouses and shorts for a sportswear firm. Within a month, Jose was employed as a street vendor, selling fruit and flowers to people in cars at busy intersections. The two older children cared for the baby while their parents were away. In February, Lupe rented a sewing machine and started working at home. Now, she could watch the baby, so the other children could go to school.

This decision solved the problem of how Lupe could continue to work without paying a baby-sitter, an expense they couldn't afford, even when Jose started to work at a car wash. It did, however, bring another problem. She was no longer paid an hourly wage, but only for the number of blouses and shorts she produced. At forty-nine cents apiece, she found that she averaged only a little over a dollar an hour. To make as much as she had been used to making, she had to work twelve to fifteen hours a day. Sometimes, when the baby was sick and needed more attention, her older children had to help her. And when her boss demanded that she produce more pieces of clothing, her children started working from the time they arrived home from school until ten o'clock at night. During summer vacation, between caring for the baby and sewing, neither child had any time left over for play, and Lupe had no time to cook. The family existed on cold cereal and sandwiches. Seven days a week, their lives were focused on the work they needed in order to survive.

THE UNCERTAIN JOURNEY

When the children returned to school in September, a lack of sleep and a lack of time to do their homework caused their grades to drop. Two months later, when their teachers told the vice principal that the formerly attentive students were falling asleep in class, he visited their home. The first week in December, Jose and Lupe received a letter with an official-looking seal on the envelope and the top of the page.

Neither Jose nor Lupe read English well enough to understand everything in the letter, but they knew it meant that they had come to the attention of the authorities. They realized it probably meant that they were going to be sent back to Ecuador, where they no longer had a home or a way to make a living. All the money they had spent, all the hardships they had endured—had they been for nothing?

When Jose had someone explain the exact meaning of the letter, he found that it contained more good news than bad. First, he was told that it was against the law for their children to work so many hours. Second, he learned that Lupe's employer should have paid much more for the work that she and the children had done.

"We have contacted your employer," the letter concluded. "He has agreed to pay you and your children $24,500, the amount owed for accumulated straight time plus all overtime hours."

Six months passed before Lupe received the check. During the wait, Jose continued to work at the car wash, and Lupe became a street vendor, selling the burritos and tamales that she made in her tiny kitchen, keeping a watchful eye on her toddler as he played

How Long Is a Row?

in a nearby corner of a park. They also consulted an attorney about getting their "green cards," documents that allow them to work without fear of being deported.

Neither Jose nor Lupe had ever dreamed of having so much money at one time. They spent many evenings deciding whether to spend it for a down payment on a house or to use it to go into business for themselves. When Jose heard of a fish market for sale in a busy downtown area, the decision was made. Now, a steady stream of customers keep both Jose and Lupe busy.

"If things keep going well," says Jose, "we'll be able to buy a home in a couple of years." The words are spoken in almost perfect English, which he learned by taking night classes in an adult school.

5

If You Want Your Children…

"My family and I are together now." Arnulfo says. *"And I pray that we will always be together. There was one time when I thought I might never see my children again. That miserable coyote . . . and to think I trusted him with my family's safekeeping."*

Arnulfo grew up in Guadalajara, Mexico. After finishing primary school, he worked with his father and mother in their small restaurant. When he was twenty, he married Maria, a girl he had known for most of his life. Within four years, they had two children, Bianca and Carlos. Since Arnulfo expected to inherit the family business, his future seemed secure.

Then, almost overnight, his situation changed: The taxes and license fees on the restaurant went up, while the people in the area were losing their jobs and had no money to spend on eating out. Arnulfo's parents finally had to sell their business to pay their debts. At their age, they had

If You Want Your Children . . .

little hope of starting another business or of finding any work. Even the young, strong Arnulfo could find no work. To make matters worse, he now had to support his parents in addition to his own family. The only solution was to travel northward to the land where it was said there were plenty of jobs for everyone.

Three months later, Arnulfo was standing on the north levee of the Tijuana River. All that separated him from southern California was an eight-foot-tall chain-link fence that was topped with three strands of barbed wire. He was only one of the scores of men and women who, since midmorning, had been watching the border patrol officers drive back and forth in their jeep. It was obvious to the uniformed officers on the United States side of the fence and also to the ragged would-be immigrants on the Mexican side that most of the immigrants would eventually win their "stare down." As soon as the jeep moved on to check another section of the border, the *sin papeles* would be over the fence and out of sight within minutes.

Now, it was time. The jeep was gone. One of the men clambered up a fence, snipped the barbed wire with a pair of clippers, and was followed by a parade of men and women. Arnulfo took a deep breath as he jumped from the fence onto the soil of *El Norte*. Here, he knew, lay the opportunities he would never have in Mexico. But here too was a land where he was a stranger and where he must keep hidden from anyone who might work for the government whose laws he had broken.

Using a combination of taxicabs and buses, by the next night Arnulfo had found his way to Pasadena, where sev-

THE UNCERTAIN JOURNEY

eral of his friends had lived for over a year. While spending the next week searching for a job, Arnulfo had an occasional moment of despair. Had he left his family for nothing? Where were all the jobs he had been told were to be found in this country?

But then one of his roommates was deported. As soon as Arnulfo heard the news, he walked to the restaurant where his friend had worked. "Pedro is gone," he said to the evening dishwasher. "Tell the *patron* I will be here tomorrow morning at five-thirty."

When the manager heard the news, he nodded. He was used to having his busboys and dishwashers disappear and, like magic, having another one appear to take his place. The *sin papeles* had an unfailing grapevine along which such news was relayed.

This breakfast shift enabled Arnulfo to take a dishwashing job in another restaurant, where he worked from 3:00 P.M. to 11:00 P.M. Every week, one of his two paychecks was sent to Guadalajara to support his family. From the other, Arnulfo paid his share of the rent and other living expenses. The money that was left over, he tucked in the back of a dresser drawer, knowing that if he was deported and didn't return, one of his roommates would mail it to him.

The two-room apartment that Arnulfo shared with five other *sin papeles* was located only three blocks from his morning job, but every day the breakfast cook picked him up in his car to take him to work. "The less you're on the streets, the better," the cook said. "Immigration agents are asking for identification from anyone who looks like a

If You Want Your Children . . .

Mexican." Arnulfo hadn't understood everything that had been said, but the words, "immigration" and "identification" were familiar to him. He also understood the manager when he came into the dishroom, pointed toward the ceiling, and said, "Get on the roof. ¡*Andale! Vamos!*" Those words meant that *la migra* was in the parking lot or coming through the back door. They meant that Arnulfo should climb onto the top of the dumpster, scramble onto the roof, and hide until he was told to come down.

Only once was Arnulfo caught in an INS "sweep." After being taken to a detention center in Los Angeles, he and a bus full of other *sin papeles* were taken to Tijuana. Three hours after his arrival in Mexico, Arnulfo was heading back to Pasadena. He missed only one day's work on both of his jobs. In each case, one of his friends had shown up to take his place. Later, when one of the busboys failed to show up for work in the second restaurant, Arnulfo asked the manager if he could have the job. The next day, he was clearing tables, offering water and coffee to the customers, and generally making the jobs of the waitresses easier. To show their appreciation for his help, at the end of the night, they each gave him three dollars.

In spite of the fact that Arnulfo was making this extra money, he continued to stay in the crowded apartment. Everyone there was content with the living arrangement. Each man paid only his small share of the rent, and each was grateful for the companionship and support of people with whom he shared a common language and background and set of experiences.

* * *

THE UNCERTAIN JOURNEY

Slowly, over the next year, Arnulfo learned to speak enough English to communicate easily with the customers and the food servers in the restaurant. One night, a customer who mistook Arnulfo for a server gave him his dinner order. Since the server was busy, Arnulfo gave the order to the cooks.

"You can do my job almost as well as I can," the server later said to him. "The next time there's an opening for a server, why don't you apply for it? You'd make a lot more money that way than you do as a busboy."

Arnulfo had seen how much money the servers made in tips. He had never thought that he would be able to have such a job, but six months later a very nervous Arnulfo was waiting on his first customers. By the time his shift had ended that night, he had made almost fifty dollars in tips—more money than he would have made in a week in Mexico.

As he walked home in the darkness of early morning, taking care to avoid the main street, ducking into an alley when a police car drove past, the germ of an idea took root in his head. Maybe I will stay in this country, he thought. Maybe I will pay a *coyote* to bring my parents and my wife and children to Pasadena. Here, my children can not only finish primary school but also high school—maybe even college. In *El Norte,* anything is possible.

By the time he reached home, he had made his decision. He would start saving all of his tips, and soon he and his family would be together, sharing the good *Americana* life. In his excitement, Arnulfo forgot, for a few moments, about the long shadow of *la migra* and the flutter of fear in

———— If You Want Your Children . . . ————

his chest whenever he saw anyone in a uniform. When he remembered, he knew that those fears would be increased five-fold when his family arrived.

No matter, he thought. Here, I have found the work that cannot be found in Mexico, so it is here I must stay. And it is proper that a man be with his family. If I can't go back to Guadalajara, they must come to Pasadena.

Almost five months passed before Arnulfo had enough money to rent a house and to bring five people from Guadalajara into Los Angeles. The *coyote*'s price was very high—three thousand dollars—but Arnulfo was willing to pay it to save his elderly parents and his wife and children the dangers and uncertainties of crossing the border by themselves.

"How long will it take?" Arnulfo asked as he handed the *coyote* his fee.

"About two or three weeks," was the reply.

As the *coyote* walked away, Arnulfo had a moment's concern. This man was a stranger, he thought. Is it possible he would take my money and give me nothing in return?

No, he decided. He is my countryman. His face is honest. He will keep his promise.

Almost two weeks passed, and Arnulfo was expecting to receive word about his family's arrival at any moment. Every time the telephone rang in the office of the restaurant, he expected his name to be called. "They're here," he imagined someone saying, and as soon as his shift was over, he would borrow a friend's car and go to Los An-

THE UNCERTAIN JOURNEY

geles to the bus depot or the train station to pick them up. His long wait would be over.

But when Arnulfo was finally called to the telephone, the message wasn't what he expected. "Your family is here," the *coyote* said. "But if you want your children, you must pay another thousand dollars."

If you want your children! The words echoed in Arnulfo's head. "But your price was three thousand dollars. I paid that. I have no more savings," he said.

"The price is now higher," replied the *coyote*. "Right now, you can pick up your wife and parents at the bus depot downtown, but you will not see your children until I get more money. I will call you again tomorrow night."

Arnulfo was overcome with a feeling of helplessness. He couldn't call the police to report this crime. If he did, they would no doubt call *la migra,* and by sunrise Arnulfo would be on a bus heading south toward the border. And then what would happen to his children? And what would happen to Maria and his parents, who at this minute were waiting for him?

The joyous family reunion, for which he had worked so hard, had become a nightmare.

When his shift was over, Arnulfo borrowed a car and drove to Los Angeles to meet Maria and his parents. When they met, they hugged one another, but their tears weren't tears of joy, they were tears of anguish. *"Mi niños, mi niños,"* Maria cried again and again.

"I'll get the money for the *coyote*," Arnulfo said. "Soon we will be all together."

―――――― *If You Want Your Children . . .* ――――――

That night was a sleepless one for Arnulfo. After taking his wife and parents to the house he had rented, he drove to his former apartment. One of his friends had just arrived home; Arnulfo's frantic knocking had awakened the others.

"I need one thousand dollars," Arnulfo said. "A *coyote* is holding Bianca and Carlos for ransom."

The men asked no questions. One by one, they went through their pockets and their wallets and handed Arnulfo the money they had available. One hundred dollars, $300, $500, $850—the pile of bills grew larger. Arnulfo himself had $75. Not quite enough. He would have to ask each of his bosses to give him an advance on his wages. Somehow, he would have to have the full amount when the *coyote* called him the next night. The lives of his children depended on it.

Two days after their arrival in Los Angeles, Bianca and Carlos were reunited with their mother and father. Three months later, the money Arnulfo had borrowed for the ransom was repaid, but he continued to work two jobs so he could save enough to make a down payment on a house. Shortly after he became a home owner, he applied for permanent resident's status, which was granted. Now, he could open a bank account. He could call the police if he needed their protection, he could take his children to a hospital if they became ill or injured; he could walk the streets, day or night, without fear of being picked up as an illegal alien.

Today, Arnulfo works only one job—he's been a waiter in the same restaurant for fifteen years. Bianca attends junior college and

THE UNCERTAIN JOURNEY

plans to become an accountant. Carlos is a senior in high school. Because of his good grades, he will be eligible for a scholarship when he goes to college.

Until Arnulfo obtained his permanent resident's status, Maria had been afraid to leave the house except to do the necessary shopping. Now, she has learned to speak English and is working as a cook for a catering company. Both she and Arnulfo are looking forward to their vacations, when they and their children will return to Guadalajara for a visit.

"Bianca and Carlos must not forget their homeland," says Arnulfo, "but we will return to Pasadena. This is where we now belong."

6

You Are Only a Boy

Francisco had just turned seven years old when his father died. A few months later, he also lost his mother. For almost five years, he lived in the teeming barrio of Colonia Libertad in Tijuana, Mexico, with his aunt and uncle and their eight children. Although he was made to feel welcome, Francisco soon came to realize that every bite of food he took meant that much less food in the stomachs of his cousins. As a day laborer, his uncle sometimes made only enough to fill a pot with beans and a few chiles. Being able to buy a chicken was a cause for celebration.

Francisco was only twelve when he and two friends decided to seek their fortunes in *El Norte*. By listening to the conversations in the plaza and bazaars, Francisco learned that the border patrol's jeeps and cars and helicopters were usually deployed in the area north of the soccer field. There, on the United States side of the border, officers stood with their binoculars trained on the *Cañon Zapata*. Although Mexicans stood as lookouts on the hill-

THE UNCERTAIN JOURNEY

tops around the canyon to alert the immigrants to the presence of patrol agents, more and more of the travelers were being prevented from entering the United States.

Since so much of the border patrol's attention was concentrated on that one section of the border, many *sin papeles* were now crossing at *el borde,* an area three miles west of the soccer field.

"It is much faster there," Francisco overheard one man say. "It sometimes takes four hours getting through the canyon. At *el borde,* you can just go through the fence and there you are in San Ysidro. Then you jump into a trolley and *vamanos,* you are gone."

To earn money for the trip, Francisco approached American tourists, offering to guard their cars against vandalism or to act as a guide to the bazaars and sports events in Tijuana. He also rummaged through the town's huge dump and found salvage, which he sold. Within a week, he had earned fifteen dollars.

Two days later, Francisco and his friends, each carrying a plastic grocery bag stuffed with a change of clothing, some food, a shoe-shining brush, some shoe polish, and their meager savings, were standing on the southern levee of the Tijuana River at *el borde.* They were only two of scores of men, women, and children who were waiting for dusk so they could slip through one of the many holes in the fence. As at the soccer field, vendors were selling food and drink, *coyotes* were peddling their services, and sharp-eyed thieves were looking for careless victims.

The concrete levee slopes up about twenty-five feet from the fifty-foot-wide river bottom. Some of the immigrants

You Are Only a Boy

were waiting at the bottom of the slope, in the trickle of water that wound its way through the channel. One enterprising man had placed boards that straddled the river halfway up the slope and was charging people a forty-cent toll for the privilege of getting across the river without getting their feet wet. Francisco and his friends elected to save their money.

As the afternoon went on, border patrol vehicles drove up and down the northern levee. Evidently, *la migra* had decided to move their forces to this new area.

"No problem," Francisco said. "We can outwait them. And if we get caught, we'll just try again later."

When the sun went down, the officers parked their jeeps. Soon, the night's friendly darkness cloaked the movements of the people massed on the Mexican side of the border. Now, Francisco thought, now is the time. His muscles tensed as he felt the crowd press forward. He took his first steps away from the poverty of his homeland.

But what was this? The area was suddenly illuminated with a ghostly glow from lights atop a series of small towers. Confused, Francisco stopped short, as did everyone else on the levee. The border patrol was using a new and unexpected weapon in their war against illegal immigration.

"There," one of Francisco's friends whispered. "Down there, outside the ring of light, we can cross. It's said that the traveling is more difficult there, but we will not be seen."

Many of the would-be immigrants had the same idea. Almost as if the light were pushing them into the shadows,

THE UNCERTAIN JOURNEY

they walked downstream. When Francisco reached the darkness, he stood still, afraid to move because he was experiencing a temporary night blindness after his exposure to the lights. Then, when his eyes had adjusted to the change, he pushed forward along with his friends and a group of *sin papeles*. His heart pounding from the excitement of the adventure, he slid down the side of the levee, sloshed through the water, scrambled up the other side, then slipped through the flimsy wire fence.

Stumbling in the darkness, Francisco followed closely upon the heels of the man directly in front of him. Soon, he was running along a road that previous immigrants had strewn with boulders to slow any pursuing vehicles. After crossing a wide field that was crisscrossed with deep ruts and that offered no shelter from the eyes of the border patrol, the group walked along the side of a highway that led to San Ysidro, hiding behind trees or in ditches whenever a car passed by. When they reached San Ysidro, it was a simple task to catch a bus to San Diego.

When the trio of friends had left Mexico, the plan had been for them to go to Los Angeles. Francisco, however, decided to stay in San Diego, where he could be less than an hour away from his aunt and uncle and his cousins. He was grateful to them for taking him in when he was orphaned. He wanted to be quickly available if any of them needed his help. In fact, his main goal in the United States, aside from his own survival, was to be able to send a little money to his relatives. He felt that his own parents would have wanted him to do that much.

You Are Only a Boy

On the morning after his arrival in the United States, Francisco made his way to downtown San Diego. Here, he picked a busy corner and set up his shoe-shining business.

"Pintarlos zapatos!" he called, waving his shoe-shining equipment at the passersby. "Shine your shoes!" The first hour he worked, he had three customers, who gave him a dollar apiece. By the end of the day, he had made fifteen dollars, more than enough to buy something to eat and to replace the shoe polish he had used. What everyone says is true, he thought. *El Norte* is indeed a wonderful place.

For two weeks, Francisco worked all day shining shoes, then after eating a hamburger or a burrito, spent the night sleeping on a bus bench or under a tree in a park. Soon, he hoped, he would be able to save enough money to rent a room and to buy some new clothes. Then he would start saving up again to send some money to his uncle. And perhaps he could buy a small transistor radio so he could listen to the music of Mexico as he waited for customers. Oh, there were so many things he could do with all the money he was making.

But then, Francisco's good luck changed to bad. One night, as he was sleeping on a picnic table in the park, rough hands shook him awake. "Give me your money," a man's voice said. Francisco didn't understand the English words, but it was clear what the robber wanted. Quickly, so as not to make the six-foot-tall man angry, Francisco handed over his savings. Just before the robber turned and ran down the path, he grabbed the bag that contained the shoe-shining equipment. "No, no," Francisco cried, but

THE UNCERTAIN JOURNEY

there was nothing he could do but watch his means of livelihood disappear into the shadows.

There was no more sleep for Francisco that night. He was frightened when a breeze caused the leaves of the trees to rustle. He was worried about being in a strange country with no money and no way to make a living. And he was suddenly very lonely.

Since he couldn't buy any more polish and brushes, Francisco started looking for a job. He soon found, though, that there was little work for a boy whose thirteenth birthday was still more than a month away. For over three weeks, he walked the streets of San Diego, stopping at every shop and hearing the same phrases: "We have no job openings" and "We do need some help, but you are only a boy. We need a grown-up person." Little by little, Francisco learned the English words that meant "There is nothing for you here. Go back to where you came from."

At night, Francisco stopped behind restaurants and markets to paw through their trash bins. Because of the wasteful ways of the *Americano* he managed to fill his stomach, but he was angry because he had come here to work and there was no work.

Francisco was beginning to think that he was going to have to return, defeated and disillusioned, to again take food from the mouths of his cousins.

Just a few days before his birthday, Francisco had almost finished going through the dumpster of a supermarket when he noticed an older woman looking at him. At first,

You Are Only a Boy

her steady gaze made him slightly fearful. Could she be *la migra*? She was walking toward him. Should he run?

No, he decided. This woman wears no uniform. She wears an old black dress, much like my aunt. I will stay where I am.

"My child, you are hungry." The woman spoke in the language of Mexico. "Have you no home?"

Francisco hesitated. The woman's eyes were full of warmth, but he knew that *la migra* might use such a person to set a trap. "Oh, yes," he replied, "of course, I have a home."

The woman opened her big woven bag, took out a pencil, and wrote something on a piece of paper. "Here, keep this address and telephone number," she said, handing the paper to Francisco. "If you need help, you can call upon me."

Francisco looked at the note, ashamed to admit that he had gone to school for only three years and had trouble reading.

"Follow me," the woman said. "I will show you where I live."

She knows I cannot read, Francisco thought as he walked beside her, keeping a safe distance between them. He wanted to be able to escape if this woman did turn out to be an immigration official.

They walked for six blocks, then turned a corner onto a residential street. "That's my house," the woman said, pointing to a rundown two-story wooden structure where there were two young boys sitting on the porch. "Don't forget. You come if you need help." She walked away. Francisco was once again alone, but he no longer felt as if he was friendless in this bustling foreign city.

A month passed, during which Francisco earned a few dollars doing yard work and running errands, slept on bus benches, and washed up in rest rooms. There was no one who would give him any work that lasted more than a few hours. Days elapsed between one job and another. More than once, he thought of the woman in the black dress and that large old house. When the rainy season started, and he could find no place to stay dry while he slept, he admitted defeat. Two hours later, he was knocking on the door of her house, from the open window of which came the aroma of fresh-baked bread and chili.

Francisco was welcomed into the home, which was a shelter for boys who had been found living on the street. At the time of his arrival, the woman in black, Mrs. Ortega, was caring for six other youths. At first, Francisco felt as he had when he had been living with his aunt and uncle—that he was taking food from the mouths of others, that he should be taking care of himself instead of being dependent. Mrs. Ortega soon convinced him that by going to school and helping in the upkeep of the house, he would be doing what was expected of him and would owe her nothing.

"In this country," Mrs. Ortega said, "you must know how to read and write English. Study hard, learn well, and one day, you will be able to help others who are in need.

You Are Only a Boy

Meanwhile, I will be your mother and the other boys, your brothers."

Five years later, Francisco became the first person in his family to graduate from high school. He then went to the local college to take a business course and graduated near the top of his class. It was when he applied for a job as loan counselor at a bank that an immigration official became aware of his illegal status. Mrs. Ortega interceded for Francisco, pointing out his excellent scholastic record and his ambition.

"He should be allowed to stay in the United States," she said to a judge during one of Francisco's court appearances. "He has worked so hard for so many years to make something of himself."

Currently, Francisco's case is being reviewed by a higher court, and the outlook is good for its favorable outcome. Meanwhile, Francisco is working as a box boy in a supermarket. Until he receives his permanent resident's status, he will not be able to take a job more suited to his college training.

7

The *Bot Pipple*

Raymond's family in Haiti had always been desperately poor, and the government under which they lived had no concern for the plight of the peasants. Many of their friends had joined the *bot pipple,* the Creole term for the emigrants who traveled to the United States in vessels that were often leaky and overcrowded.

But Raymond's parents had never become desperate enough to send one of their five sons on such a dangerous journey. They were able to eke out a living by working on the cotton and coffee plantations during planting and harvest seasons, by growing vegetables on their small plot of land, and by catching fish. And, like most poor Haitians, they had several pigs rooting about in the mud yard behind their primitive wood-frame hut. To the peasants, owning a few pigs was the same as having money in a bank. During times of economic crisis, one of the creatures could be slaughtered and the money from the sale of the meat used to tide the family over.

The Bot Pipple

"As long as we have two or three pigs," said Raymond's father, "we will be all right." Even when there was an extreme emergency, he made sure that there was a litter of baby pigs on the way before he killed an adult pig. In this way, he felt assured that his "savings account" would not be depleted.

That assurance disappeared in 1981. In order to stem the epidemic of swine fever that had swept over the island, the government ordered the peasants to kill all their pigs. Raymond and his father led a revolt aimed at letting the healthy pigs live, but when soldiers entered their village and threatened them with jail, they had to comply with the unfair law. Raymond's mother wept and moaned, "My pigs. Give me back my pigs."

Raymond's father was deeply concerned about the loss of his only wealth, but he was more worried about the possible consequences of being involved in the short-lived revolt. He decided to send Raymond, his eldest son, to the United States. There, Raymond could avoid the possibility of becoming a political prisoner, and he could also find a job and send money back to his family.

Once the decision was made, the entire family cooperated in the financing of Raymond's trip. One uncle sold his land and his house with its mud-daubed walls, then built a crude shelter for himself, his wife, and his two children on the land owned by Raymond's father. Another uncle donated the money he had raised from the sale of one of his two cows, and an aunt gave the proceeds of the sale of her handmade pots. Meanwhile, Raymond's parents were picking plantains and harvesting sugarcane in order to help feed the relatives who were making these sacrifices.

When Raymond's father had made inquiries about the cost of a trip to the United States, he was told it could be as low as one hundred dollars or as high as two thousand dollars. After four months, during which the family had collected four hundred dollars, it was decided that it was time for Raymond to go to Port de Paix on the northern coast of Haiti. There were many tears shed by the women, because it was well known that along the route to Florida, there were sharks that were fat from eating the bodies of countless boat people.

Seventeen-year-old Raymond, however, was looking forward to his adventure. He bundled up a change of clothing, a Bible, a photograph of his parents and his brothers, a bottle of water, stalks of sugarcane, and some dry sheets of cassava bread. For two days and two nights, he walked northward. When he reached the coast, he went to a small café where he was to look for a certain boat owner who was said to charge a fair price for transportation to Florida. Not only that, Raymond had been told that this Mr. Lemonge was an honest man, unlike others who collected their fees, then later killed their passengers, dumped their bodies into the water, and returned to Haiti to collect more money from more desperate people.

Outside the café, Raymond found a crowd of men and women who were waiting to negotiate with the various boat owners. Raymond went from person to person, asking for Mr. Lemonge, until an elderly man took him by the arm and led him to a table at the back of the café.

The Bot Pipple

Raymond waited until the people ahead of him had struck their deals after a few hastily spoken words and an exchange of money.

"I wish to go to Florida," Raymond said to the tanned, burly man seated at the table.

"Ah, you and hundreds of others," said Mr. Lemonge, grinning. "The price is three hundred fifty dollars, and we sail at midnight tonight."

Only three hundred fifty dollars! That leaves me with fifty dollars, Raymond thought. I am fortunate, indeed. After receiving instructions on where to board the boat, he hoisted his pack on his back and walked outside to sit in the sun and wait for the time for departure.

A little after midnight, with the clouds covering the crescent moon, Raymond and about fifty other emigrants crowded onboard an aging sailing vessel that was manned by Mr. Lemonge and a crew of one. Even to a person as inexperienced with seafaring as Raymond, it was evident that the boat was greatly overcrowded. The passengers sat elbow to elbow in a space that had been made for no more than twenty. Still, aside from the discomfort caused by the lack of room, the first hour of the trip across the Windward Passage was uneventful. Then the waves grew stronger and rocked the boat until the passengers started praying that they would not become meals for the sharks that were following them. The vessel tipped, and one of the women seated near the rail would have gone overboard but for the hands that reached for her and pulled her to safety. Just moments later, a wave tossed a shadowy hulk toward the

THE UNCERTAIN JOURNEY

vessel. Raymond could have almost reached out and touched the object, which he realized was an empty boat that had missed them by only a few feet.

"How many people lost their lives on that vessel?" murmured the man sitting next to Raymond. "Will we perhaps suffer the same fate?"

Raymond did not answer. His mind was too full of visions of sharks and of the blackness of water, and his stomach was bitterly complaining about the last meal he had eaten. He clutched his belongings to him, shut his eyes, and prayed that he would be alive to see the light of morning.

When the sun rose, the weary passengers were greeted by the welcome sight of land just ahead of them. Within a half hour, Mr. Lemonge had docked his vessel at a Cuban port, where Raymond was glad to disembark and stretch his legs and feel solid earth under his feet. Dockhands gave everyone some water and a small meal, but their hospitality was marred by their obvious wish to send these intruders on their way as soon as possible. Raymond hardly had time to gulp his food before he was told to board the boat again.

For most of the next two days, the boat people were blessed with calm seas and favorable winds, but Raymond was made aware of the dangers of the journey by the occasional sight of a small boat drifting unattended. And as they approached the Florida coast, Mr. Lemonge reminded them that they had yet one more possible obstacle to face. "The United States Coast Guard patrols will be looking

The Bot Pipple

for us," he said. "We must be watchful and finish our journey under cover of darkness. When we are near the shore, I will give a signal. You must then jump overboard and swim the rest of the way. When you reach land, find a hiding spot right away. The border patrol has many eyes. If you are caught, you will be put into a prison camp. Behind barbed wire you will be of no help to your families."

Raymond had heard about one of those prisons where his countrymen were held for months while awaiting deportation. I can't let myself be caught, he thought. My family will starve without my help.

That night, as he prepared to leave the boat to enter the cold, choppy water, he thought again of his family and how they had sacrificed everything to send him to the United States. He strapped his bundle of possessions securely to his back, and when it was his turn to jump, he took a deep breath, then joined the other boat people as they swam toward shore. Silently, with strong even strokes, Raymond closed the gap between the boat and the land. He was only about fifty feet from shore when he heard a fellow immigrant gasping and thrashing about a short distance behind him.

Someone's in trouble, he thought. But I'm so close to safety. I can't stop to help. I must think only of my family. Already, the swiftest swimmers had stumbled out of the water and were scrambling to get out of sight of any beach patrol officers.

But after taking a few more strokes, Raymond reversed directions and went toward the shadowy figure that was

THE UNCERTAIN JOURNEY

now sinking below the surface of the water. He grabbed a handful of hair, then with the stranger in tow, again struck out for shore. A few moments later, he was dragging the man up onto the beach, and another immigrant was running toward them to offer his help.

"He's breathing," he said to Raymond. "Now, quickly, we must leave or we will be caught."

Raymond hesitated. This man had almost drowned. Shouldn't he stay to make sure he was all right? Then the figure on the sand by his feet stirred, opened his eyes, and sat up. Raymond pulled him to his feet, and gripping his arm, headed for the low wall that separated the beach from the highway. After shoving his companion over the wall, he leaped over it himself.

He wasn't a moment too soon. Just as he crouched down, Raymond spotted the headlights of a vehicle traveling at a high speed in their direction. Shivering in his wet clothes, he waited until the vehicle had passed them and the sound of the engine had died down. He and his new companion then ran to the back of a closed gas station, where Raymond opened his pack and changed into his dry clothing. Henri, his companion, had lost his pack. He would have to wait until the sun rose before he would stop shivering.

Raymond and Henri spent the next morning walking along the highway, jumping for cover whenever a car passed by. At each small farm, they stopped and asked for work, but too many immigrants had been there before them and all the jobs were taken. As all of their food was

The Bot Pipple

gone, Raymond stopped at a small store and bought some bread, lunch meat, and soda pop. When he saw how much he had to pay for so little, he realized that here in the United States, his money would soon be gone. If he did not find work soon, he might well be as hungry as those he had left behind in Haiti.

As the two travelers walked down an alley behind a grocery store in a small town, a young man was emptying some discarded fruit and vegetables in a dumpster. Raymond and Henri had the same thought at the same moment. After waiting for the store's employee to leave, they walked toward the dumpster and began retrieving wilted heads of lettuce and bruised apples. In their excitement, they didn't notice that the employee had walked out of the store's back door carrying some cartons.

"Hey, there!" the young man called when he saw the two travelers. Clutching their food, Raymond and Henri turned to run.

"Wait! Perhaps I can help you."

At the sound of the voice, Raymond stopped, but distrustful, did not approach the stranger. Henri stood close behind him.

"I am Auguste. Just a few months ago, I was as you are now," the stranger said. "I can tell you where to find friends."

Raymond still did not move, but neither did he try to escape. "Where are these friends?" he asked.

"Go to a town called Belle Glade—it's on a big lake about a day's walk from here. Many Haitians live there, and perhaps they know where the jobs are."

THE UNCERTAIN JOURNEY

After thanking Auguste, Raymond and Henri followed his instructions. By the time the sun set the next day, they had reached Belle Glade, where thousands of immigrants lived in barracks made of cement blocks and in rooming houses with floors of sagging plywood. Here, the discouraged travelers spent the night sleeping on the ground behind a dilapidated trailer. The next morning, the inhabitants of the trailer shared their meager breakfast with them.

Even with the help of their newfound friends, Raymond and Henri did not find any work for almost a month. During the past year, tens of thousands of Haitians had arrived in Florida, and still more were landing daily. Although many were caught by the border patrol and put into detention camps, many more fled into the Florida countryside. For every job available, there were twenty people waiting to fill it. Sometimes the immigrants had nothing to eat but the rotting leftover vegetables in the fields, or the food that some church workers brought to them once a week.

At last, just when Raymond had spent the last of his money, he and Henri were hired to pick winter vegetables. They worked twelve to fifteen hours a day and spent their nights in a labor camp, sleeping outdoors on the filthy blankets they'd been given as bedding. Still, it was work, and Raymond and Henri were grateful for the opportunity to earn two to three dollars a day.

When that job was done, they became part of the meandering migrant stream that worked its way northward, stopping at citrus groves, vegetable farms, and sugarcane

The Bot Pipple

fields just long enough to help with the harvest, then moving on to the next crop.

The days were long and the work was grueling, but every month, when Raymond mailed a money order to Haiti, he felt that he was succeeding in the mission he had been given. His family would survive.

As the years passed, Raymond continued to take pride in the fact that because of him his family had enough to eat and his parents could pay the fees that allowed his brothers to remain in school. Still, he had much reason to be worried about the safety of his relatives. Whenever he met a newly arrived refugee from his homeland, he was told of the killings of innocent people by soldiers who acted on orders from the Haitian leaders. Raymond's goal now went beyond keeping the members of his family fed. He would not be happy until they had joined him in the United States. The first step toward that goal was taken when he applied for amnesty under the new federal program.

Because he was now a temporary legal resident, he had the courage to leave the migrant stream and take a job as a janitor in a factory in Charleston, South Carolina. Here, he was paid only five dollars an hour, but the work was steady and he was able to attend a trade school at night. A year later, he was qualified to take a job as a mechanic. Since his wages were now double what they had been, he started a savings account.

It took over two years, during which he shared a tenement apartment with five other immigrants, but the day

THE UNCERTAIN JOURNEY

came when he was able to arrange transportation for his parents and his brothers. The boat they would be traveling on was in good repair, and the captain was trustworthy. During the journey, their lives would not be in danger, as Raymond's had been.

Raymond's relatives arrived safely in the United States. Now they all have jobs and are living in a large rented house. Although each of them occasionally dreams about returning to their homeland, they all know that such a move would be unwise. There the soil is too poor to grow a good crop, and there are few jobs available for mechanics.

An even more important reason is that although the regime under which they lived for so many years has been overthrown, there is still much political instability. The memory of gunfire in the streets and of innocent people being dragged off to prison where they were left to die is still fresh in the minds of every Haitian immigrant.

It is this memory that caused Raymond to go to an attorney to receive help in applying for political asylum for the members of his family. If he can prove that they would face persecution or death if they return to Haiti, there is a chance that they will be able to become legal residents of the United States. Meanwhile, at home, whenever there is a knock at their door, they must peek out to see who their visitor is, and at work, they must be ready to run if an official-looking stranger appears.

8

He Will Give Me Sanctuary

So many lights—they go on for miles and miles. Chicago must be the biggest city in the United States. I could get lost in there. The thoughts flashed through Luisa's mind as the jet slowed and circled the airport, preparing for landing. And then the thoughts were blotted out by fear—the same fear that had gripped her when the plane had left Mexico City and that had stayed with her in varying degrees all during the long flight. *What will happen to my children if the plane crashes and I die?* she wondered. *Will my sister be able to care for them?*

Please, let me survive, she prayed silently. Let me live so I can support my family.

It wasn't until she felt the jet's wheels touch the ground that Luisa released her grip on the armrests of the seat. The journey was over. She was alive. And soon, she'd be working for a rich family who would give her plenty of food and a room of her own, something she'd never had before. And most important—they would give her a good wage.

THE UNCERTAIN JOURNEY

Even after she made her payments on the loan she had taken out to pay her *coyote,* she would have enough to send money to her home in Nicaragua. With it, her sister could buy oranges and milk and sometimes a piece of meat for her own children and for Luisa's two children. And when it was time for school, she could buy them shoes and new dresses and trousers.

School. I won't be there to see my children off to their classes, Luisa thought. A wave of homesickness swept over her, and she cursed the fate that had caused her to leave her family. Then she brushed away the tears that filled her eyes, and scolded herself for being an ungrateful wretch. Forgive me, she prayed. Thanks to the opportunity you have seen fit to give me, my little ones will no longer be hungry. She vowed that as soon as possible, she would go to church and give thanks in a proper way.

By now, the plane had rolled to a stop. Luisa clutched the cloth bag that contained a change of clothing plus the tourist visa that her *coyote* had helped her obtain. Right now, she was in the United States legally. After she took a job, though, she would be living in fear of deportation.

Luisa followed the other passengers off the plane, along a corridor, and into a massive building. Here, everywhere she looked, people were greeting each other and laughing and talking in a language she couldn't understand. Never in her life had she felt more alone. Never had she been more frightened.

Following her *coyote*'s instructions, she reached into her coat pocket and took out a red bandana, which she tied around her head in the style of the peasants. She then

He Will Give Me Sanctuary

walked past the area where people were waiting for their baggage and went outside. Here, she saw the island where people waited for the buses that came and went with a roar and a puff of black smoke. "Wait on the center island," the *coyote* had said. "Someone will come for you. That person will ask you what your name is, then he will take you to the home of Mr. and Mrs. Cooper."

Thirty minutes passed, and people went back and forth and around Luisa, but no one stopped and spoke to her. Her fear turned to panic. What if my employers don't appear? she wondered. I have no money to return home. Where will I go? What will I do? The wind turned colder and she shivered in her thin coat. Ten minutes later, a short thin man approached her. "Are you Luisa Mendez?" he asked in Spanish.

Relief swept through Luisa. "*Si, si,*" she replied.

"I'm Eleseo," the man said. "I will take you to the Coopers."

Such a large house for only two people, Luisa kept saying to herself the first week she worked for the Coopers. The front room itself appeared to have twice as much space as the entire house where she and her two children had lived. Luisa had to work all day, every day just to keep the house clean and to do the cooking for the Coopers and their various friends who came to dinner several times a week.

Luisa didn't mind the work, because at home she had always worked hard. But she didn't like the isolation, the loneliness, the homesickness that haunted her every waking hour. If she and Eleseo had not taken hurried meals together in the kitchen, she would have had no one to talk to in her own language. He also was from Nicaragua and had worked for the Coopers for three years as their gardener, handyman, and sometimes chauffeur—anything that needed to be done. It was Eleseo who drove her to church every Sunday morning. It was here, in the spacious sanctuary, that she gained the strength to make it through another week.

Once a month, Eleseo also took her to the post office, where she mailed a letter and a money order to her sister. These trips to the church and to the post office were the only times Mrs. Cooper allowed her to leave the house.

She didn't protest the lack of freedom until the day she received a letter from her mother saying that Rigoberto, one of her cousins, was now living in Chicago too. When she asked for a few hours off to visit with him, the answer was a firm no.

"It's for your own protection, dear," Mrs. Cooper replied in her broken Spanish. "When you're in my home, you're safe from the immigration officers. When you're on the street or in a restaurant, you are not." She paused. "You wouldn't want to be sent back to Nicaragua, would you? How would you support your children?"

"You are right, of course," Luisa said, grateful for Mrs. Cooper's concern. It wasn't until later that evening that she admitted to herself that, even with her comfortable room, her television set, and her good wages, she was beginning to think of her employers more as jailers than as protectors. She looked at the small blurred picture of her children that lay on the table beside her bed. *"Mi niños,"* she murmured. "My little ones. When will I see you again?" Give me strength so I can endure, she prayed. And then she cried herself to sleep.

The ache in Luisa's heart grew stronger as two Christmases came and went and another new year advanced into summer. If I could go home for only a few days, just to see how my children have grown, just to tell them how much I love them, Luisa thought. One afternoon, she found Mrs. Cooper in the garden clipping some roses.

"Have you put the roast in the oven?" Mrs. Cooper asked. "Tonight, you must serve dinner by five-thirty."

"Yes," Luisa replied, then paused, trying to remember the English words for what she wanted to say. "Please, I wish to have a *vacacion,* a short time to visit Nicaragua. My cousin will loan me the money."

"But, my dear, how would I manage without you?" Mrs. Cooper said.

"It would be only for a short time," Luisa said. "I need to see my children."

"And have you thought about how you'll get back here? How will you cross the border without papers? I understand the immigration people are all over the airports now."

Luisa knew Mrs. Cooper was right. To leave the country now might mean that all the sacrifices she'd already made would be for nothing.

―――― THE UNCERTAIN JOURNEY ――――

* * *

When Luisa had come to the United States, her first goal had been to pay off her debt. In less than two years, that goal was reached, and she started doubling the amount of money she sent to her sister each payday. Now, in a bank in Nicaragua, there was a savings account that was steadily growing. When she had saved enough to buy a sewing machine, to pay for her transportation back home, and to support her family until her sewing business took root, Luisa planned to return to her family.

Two more years, Luisa thought. If all goes well, it will take only two more years.

But then one afternoon, while Luisa was dusting the dining room, the doorbell rang and Mrs. Cooper went to answer it. "Yes?" Luisa heard her say.

"Mrs. Ronald Cooper?" a man asked.

"Yes."

"I'm Harold Robinson with the Immigration and Naturalization Service. I understand you employ a maid."

"Why, yes, but . . ."

¡Inmigración! Luisa didn't wait to hear any more of the conversation. If she were sent back to Nicaragua now, she would have only a little more than when she left—no sewing machine, no way to support her family. Running to her room, she grabbed her bag, stuffed some clothes and the picture of her children into it, and ran out of the kitchen door. Across the yard, out the back gate, down the street—she didn't know where she was going, only that she had to escape from this Harold Robinson.

And then she knew where she could go—to the big

He Will Give Me Sanctuary

church where she found peace every Sunday, where there were others who spoke her language, most of them illegal aliens like herself. The priest! Luisa knew that he had helped others. She knew he would help her. He would give her sanctuary.

By six o'clock that evening, Father Pedro had introduced Luisa to a group of *sin papeles* who were being temporarily housed in a building next to the church. "You will stay here with us as long as necessary," he said. "We will also help you find work. Perhaps there is a parishioner who needs a housekeeper."

For the briefest of moments, Luisa thought about Mrs. Cooper and the company she had invited for dinner that night. Who would cook? Who would serve? But her tinge of guilt vanished when she realized that if she had not fled, she would at this moment be in a detention center. Within days, she would have been on a plane headed southward, hardly any better off than when she left, with nothing to look forward to but a lifetime of poverty.

After she had been assigned a cot, Luisa called Rigoberto to let him know where she was. Rigoberto told her not to worry.

"Father Pedro will take good care of you. He has helped many of our countrymen. And I think I know someone who may have a job for you."

Luisa had been staying next door to the church for only two weeks when Father Pedro told the group that he had to close his shelter. "I've fought against this moment for many months," he said. "Now there is no more money to buy food and pay the rent on this house. And the city officials are threatening me with jail. They say that I am breaking the law by harboring people who have no permission to be in this country."

He paused. "But this is not to be the last of the matter. There are many people with big hearts in this city. Sometime soon, with their help, I will open another shelter. Meanwhile, I'll do all I can to help you find jobs and places to live."

I'll call Rigoberto, Luisa thought. He is family. He will help me.

By noon the next day, Luisa was staying in a rundown hotel in a curtained-off part of the room that Rigoberto shared with two other men. Two weeks passed before one of the men told her about an office-cleaning business that was advertising for workers. She applied for and got a job. When she received her first paycheck, she paid her share of the rent and food and sent the rest of the money to her sister. With the money order, she enclosed a note explaining her change of address.

"I no longer have a television and a soft bed," she wrote. "But I am happy to have found another job so quickly." She said nothing about the cockroaches and the rats that scuttered about in the darkness. After all, in Nicaragua there were also vermin.

Luisa remained grateful for the work, but it was a struggle to support herself and send money home with the two dollars an hour she was paid. Within a short time, she had taken an additional job as a maid in a motel. Her hours at her first job—seven to midnight—enabled her to sleep a few hours before reporting to work for her second job at 7:00 A.M.

The tips that many motel customers left for her were always a pleasant surprise to Luisa. Added to her hourly wage, they enabled her to pay her rent and personal expenses, so she could send all her office-cleaning paycheck to her sister.

When Luisa first started working at the motel, she was amazed to discover how wasteful the *Americanos* were. They bought chicken and tacos and pizza, ate only half of the food, and left the rest for her to throw away along with the greasy napkins and paper bags and boxes. Perhaps people who can afford to travel and stay in a motel have never been hungry, Luisa thought. If they had been, they would take the food with them and eat it later.

Six months after Luisa had moved in with Rigoberto, she came home one afternoon to find that immigration agents had "swept" the hotel and had taken at least half the tenants into custody. Rigoberto and her other roommates were among them. For three days, Luisa dreaded coming home to the empty room, cringed at the sound of each footstep in the hall, slept restlessly as she wondered what was going to happen to her now that she was alone.

Her most immediate concern was how she was going to pay the entire three hundred dollars a month rent by herself. As soon as she found the time, she went to the church to talk to Father Pedro. He introduced her to Maria, a young Guatemalan girl who had recently arrived in the United States and who had been working on a factory

THE UNCERTAIN JOURNEY

assembly line for two weeks. The next day, Maria moved in with Luisa. That night, Luisa slept well for the first time since she had come home to find Rigoberto gone.

Eighteen months passed, during which Luisa and Maria moved from the hotel into a one-bedroom house. Their landlord was Segundo, a man in his forties whose parents had come from Guatemala. Since he had been born in the United States, he was a citizen. The friendship between Segundo and Luisa slowly grew into a romance, and almost a year and a half after they met, they were married.

The marriage made Luisa more comfortable financially—she was able to quit her office-cleaning job—but it did not change her status as an illegal alien, and it caused her to miss her children even more. Segundo understood how she felt. Shortly after they were married, he told Father Pedro about Luisa's unhappiness. Father Pedro introduced him to an attorney who specialized in helping illegal aliens with their legal problems.

It has been almost a year since the attorney filed the first papers in his effort to reunite Luisa and her children. He is also trying to gain permanent resident's status for Luisa.

Segundo once suggested that he and Luisa fly to Nicaragua for a short visit with Luisa's children, but their attorney has warned them of the possibility that Luisa might not be allowed back into the United States.

"Be patient," he said. "It shouldn't be too much longer before your children will be able to come to you."

Luisa tries to be patient, but as the days and weeks pass, she finds it more and more difficult. Without the compassion of Father

He Will Give Me Sanctuary

Pedro and the support of Segundo, at times the waiting would be unbearable. Every time she is paid, she puts money into a special savings account for her children's education. I'm doing this for you, my little ones, she says to herself.

Not too long ago, Luisa dreamed of nothing more than getting her daughter through primary school and her son through high school. Now, she can dream about them going to college. If that dream becomes reality, all the years of sacrifice will have been worth it.

9

The Desert Will Bite You, Scratch You, or Poison You

Even before he approached the border of the United States, Alfredo had overcome tremendous obstacles. After leaving his homeland, Guatemala, he had walked hundreds of miles, forded dozens of rivers, and spent days and nights in wheezing creaky buses that climbed like snails up the sides of mountains, then plunged down the other side as if they would never stop. As he traveled through Mexico, he had to avoid the Mexican police, who would have either put him in jail or sent him back to Central America.

He had interrupted his journey only a few times, to earn enough pesos to buy a meal or two. He was on his way to Phoenix, Arizona, where he had heard he could make a good wage as a fruit picker. To get to Phoenix, he had to save as much money as possible to pay someone to act as a guide.

To earn money, he haunted bus and train stations and the parking lots of expensive restaurants and hotels, scur-

The Desert Will Bite You, Scratch You, or Poison You

rying around, looking for opportunities to carry luggage, then gratefully accepting the tips that the tourists offered. One afternoon, he knocked on the back door of a restaurant and asked to borrow a bucket and a sponge. Without question, the dishwasher gave them to him. Alfredo spent the next hour washing the dust and grime off the large late model cars that were parked in the lot. When their owners came out, they were all pleasantly surprised. Some of them showed their gratitude by giving Alfredo a dollar or two for his trouble.

Now, at last, he had almost reached his goal—that of crossing into the United States and finding a job that would pay him many times the two dollars a day he had made in a shoe factory in his homeland. He was sitting in a bus station in Nogales, holding a blanket and a coat and a woven sack that contained an extra shirt and a loaf of bread. Perched upon his head was a wide-brimmed straw hat. On his feet were his ragged sandals. These articles of clothing, plus dirt-encrusted canvas pants and a cotton or flannel shirt, set the *pollos* apart from the well-dressed tourists who came to this Mexican border town for a holiday weekend.

A man wearing cowboy boots and jeans came through the door of the bus station, and there was a stirring among the waiting men as he approached them. "Where are you going?" The man spoke quietly, and his question was aimed at no one in particular. Alfredo waited for someone else to answer. The gray-haired man sitting next to him shrugged and said, "Nowhere."

THE UNCERTAIN JOURNEY

"Well, if you happen to know anyone who wants to cross to the other side, I have some friends who can help," the man with the cowboy boots said.

Alfredo took a deep breath. "I know such a person," he said.

"How far does he want to go?" The *coyote*'s eyes narrowed as he looked at Alfredo.

"Phoenix."

"That costs six hundred dollars."

His price was too high for the amount of money that Alfredo had tucked in the packet that was pinned to the inside of his waistband. He shook his head. The *coyote* moved on to bargain with another *pollo*.

Within two hours, three more *coyotes* had approached the group of men who were waiting to cross the border. Each time, the price was more than Alfredo could pay. Finally, a short, thin man said his price for passage to Phoenix was four hundred dollars, a sum which Alfredo could afford.

"My name is Joaquin," said the man. "Wait here. Within an hour, I will return."

Alfredo turned and looked at the clock on the wall. It was almost midnight. Before talking to Joaquin, he had been tired. Now, he was full of energy and anxious to continue his journey. He was also slightly fearful. To strike a bargain with a *coyote* meant that he carried a large sum of money. A thief may have heard their conversation. From now on, there could be no more sleep, no walking about in the jostling crowd, no leaving the safety of the building.

The Desert Will Bite You, Scratch You, or Poison You

He got up, bought a package of potato chips, then sat back down to wait.

True to his word, Joaquin returned a little after 1:00 A.M. "Come with me," he said, motioning toward the door.

The night air was chill as Alfredo stepped onto the street. He put on his coat, feeling for his packet of money as he did so. It was still there, safe, waiting to be used for continuing his journey. He followed Joaquin down the street, then boarded a waiting bus and took a seat. Joaquin talked to the driver, then walked down the aisle, collecting his fee from each of his *pollos*.

A few minutes later, the bus was moving through the night. For three hours, Alfredo slept fitfully, vaguely aware of the grinding of gears, and of the potholes and ridges in the country roads over which they moved, and of the colicky cry of a baby in the front of the bus. There was a quick stop at a gas station, during which vendors boarded the bus to sell burritos, chicken, and corn on the cob. Alfred bought a piece of chicken and some fried potatoes.

The darkness of the sky was changing to the dusky light of morning when they arrived in the tiny town of Sonorita on the Arizona border. The passengers stepped out, shivering as the frigid north wind bit them, huddling together as Joaquin gave the bus driver some money. He then led his *pollos* down a road and across a bridge that spanned a stream. Single file, they continued across the lush floodplain with its trees, shrubs, and grass, where cows and goats were grazing. Here, seemingly unmindful of the animals, there were groups of people, some sleeping under their blankets, some stirring into wakefulness, a few rebuilding their campfires.

Joaquin asked a few of the early risers if they wanted to use him as a guide. Three of them shook their heads, saying that they had already arranged their passage to *El Norte*. Four of them agreed to join his group.

"We must now go back to town to get a few supplies," Joaquin said. "To go unprepared to face the perils of the desert is to seek death. It is an unfriendly place. Everything there will bite you, scratch you, or poison you."

Within the next hour, Alfredo exchanged some of his few remaining dollars for two gallon plastic jugs of water, a flashlight, and some food—tortillas, cheese, fried pork rinds, a can of tuna, and a can of chiles. He then rummaged through a trash can and found two plastic bags that he wound into ropes and threaded through the handles of his water jugs so he could carry them over his shoulder.

By the time the shopping was done, a scattering of American tourists had arrived in town to buy trinkets in the bazaars and exotic foods in the open-air markets. As they laughed and chattered and handed a seemingly endless supply of dollars to the merchants, they appeared unaware of the shabby silent group of *pollos* who were gathering to walk back across the bridge.

The stream meandered in great curves, and as Joaquin strode briskly along its banks, he took advantage of every shortcut. He and the *pollos* scrambled over the arroyo, slipping on rocks and loose sand, grabbing for roots to

The Desert Will Bite You, Scratch You, or Poison You

steady themselves, then walking across flat land to meet up with the stream somewhere else. Alfredo realized that many hundreds of people had traveled this route—the damp sandy bank was filled with human footprints mixed with those of animals.

Just before noon, they left the stream and climbed the north bank. Here the men had to pick their way across a parched field crisscrossed with deep fissures and with loose soil, which made for slow walking. Suddenly, just ahead of them was *la frontera,* the border. Joaquin waved to them to stay low, out of sight of any probing eyes. To remain invisible, they first crawled through an irrigation ditch, then along a barbed wire fence with a wall of tumbleweeds stuck to it.

Slowly, carefully, Joaquin led them to the highway and waited for two cars to approach and depart. Following the *coyote's* directions, the *pollos* abandoned their single-file positions and sprinted across the road. On the other side, they were confronted by a two-strand barbed wire fence. Joaquin and another man stepped on the bottom strand and lifted the top one, making a hole through which the others could slip through, one at a time.

A few hundred feet further on, there was another fence. This one was sagging so badly that each man could push it down and step right over it. Now, there was the side of a hill to climb, then still another fence, four-stranded with tightly bound vertical wires every foot or two. Although it was only four feet high, it was difficult to pass over. As Alfredo straddled it, his pants were torn and his thighs painfully pricked.

THE UNCERTAIN JOURNEY

With this final barrier out of the way, the men were able to move quickly through the hilly, uncultivated countryside. The heat from the sun pressed down upon Alfredo's back, and sweat rolled from his forehead into his eyes. As the group made its way across the burning sand, the cactus plants that dotted the area grew progressively taller, until they towered over the men. Scattered on the ground were other types of cactus, such as barrel and prickly pear. Late in the afternoon, one of the travelers was careless and ended up with needlelike spikes stuck into the parts of his feet that were left exposed by his sandals. While Joaquin paced back and forth in front of him, he sat down and slowly and painfully pulled them out.

Thirty minutes later, the group was heading toward a mountain range, the jagged line of which was barely visible against the darkening sky. For the next hour and a half, Joaquin kept a flashlight pointed at the ground in front of his feet. Alfredo felt the pull on his legs as the surface of the desert began to rise, and he was grateful when Joaquin announced that they would stop for a short break.

The men all sat down and took a few gulps from their water jugs. Alfredo lay on his back and looked up at the hundreds of stars in the black sky. Too soon, he heard the order to get to his feet and continue the journey. Standing, he took a few steps, stretched, and swung his arms around to limber them up.

"Ay," he cried as his arm was filled with points of pain. He had struck the spines of a jumping chollo cactus. With

The Desert Will Bite You, Scratch You, or Poison You

just the slightest touch, the clusters of microscopic barbs bury themselves in skin, clothing, or shoes.

"Be still," Joaquin said. "Any movement causes them to work their way further in." He reached into his knapsack and pulled out a pair of small pliers. "Here, we must use this to pull them out. They will find their way into hands or gloves."

Alfredo did not flinch as one by one Joaquin took out the needles. It would not be manly to show pain, and besides, his torn bloody skin would rouse little sympathy. Because of his carelessness, their trip was being delayed.

An hour later, the group stopped for a meal, then spent the night under a low outcropping of rock. The flames of the campfire soon turned to embers, and the cold crept into Alfredo's bones. Soon, exhaustion overtook him and he slept.

Four hours later, as the rising sun chased the darkness from the sky, Alfredo was awakened by the stirring of the men around him. Some of the men ate bread and cheese for breakfast. Alfredo ate a few pork rinds. Just a few minutes later, Joaquin called *"¡Vamos!"* and started walking toward the mountain pass. No one disputed his order. Ready or not, they all gathered their belongings together, fell into line, and followed him.

The sun rose in a cloudless sky as the men trudged through the gullies and arroyos that had been etched out by rain. Here the walking was more difficult, and they had to share the space with spiders, rats, and snakes, but they were well hidden from *la migra*. Judging from the number of discarded empty cigarette packages, candy and gum wrappers, and flashlight batteries, many people had used these passages. And many of them had died on this merciless desert floor, where the temperature was known to reach 150 degrees. Already, although the morning was still young, the sun's heat was becoming oppressive.

"In 1980," Joaquin said, "thirteen Salvadorans perished of thirst just a short way from here. They knew nothing of the desert. They were carrying heavy suitcases like tourists on a holiday."

The path to the pass grew steeper, and the vegetation became sparse. "*Andale,*" Joaquin said. "Move fast, or *la migra* might see us." Despite the crumbly surface, each man climbed like a mountain goat. Finally they reached the top of the pass and started their descent as hawks rode the air currents above them. And then came the sound that every *sin papeles* dreads—the drone of a small plane heading in their direction. With no shrubbery to hide them, the men scrambled toward the arroyo at the bottom of the pass. Alfredo was among the first to reach it. Without looking, he jumped in and found himself facing a much more imminent danger than being picked up by the border patrol—he was staring directly into the eyes of a rattlesnake that was coiling for a strike.

Frozen in fear, he stood like a statue while another man grabbed a stick, picked up the snake, and hurled it upward, out of the arroyo. "*Gracias,*" Alfredo mumbled, knowing there was no proper way to thank someone for saving his life. Grinning, the man slapped Alfredo on his back.

After a fifteen-minute meal break, Joaquin again stood

The Desert Will Bite You, Scratch You, or Poison You

up and gave the signal to move. As the men walked in a ditch, the hot, dry wind parched their skin and dried their throats, but since their water supply was now low, they allowed themselves only an occasional sip. Alfredo wondered what they would do when the life-giving liquid was completely gone.

He needn't have worried. A half hour later, Joaquin stopped by an abandoned well and told the smallest member of the group to climb down the steps that had been built on the wall of the well. Thirty feet down, he found water and called for someone to drop a water jug down. One by one the jugs were filled, two by two they were carried up to the surface.

Supplied with plenty of water but a dwindling amount of food, the group started out again. By the time the sun started to set, they had climbed two more mountains and were once again on the flat desert floor with a highway shimmering in the heat less than a mile ahead of them. Joaquin led them to an arroyo near the side of that highway.

"Here we will wait for the Indians. Maybe they will come today, maybe tomorrow," he said. "They will give us a ride to Phoenix."

Alfredo joined the others in the bottom of the arroyo. Sitting, knees tucked up, backs bent forward, they settled down to wait for whatever happened next. If they had any questions to ask Joaquin, they went unspoken. If they worried about whether or not the Indians would ever show up, their faces gave no indication of any such concern.

The frigid night arrived, and the men sought warmth

under their blankets. At dawn, they awoke, ate a small meal, stood up to stretch, then again sat down to wait, hidden from the drivers of the vehicles that occasionally passed them. Finally, about two hours later, a truck approached, slowed, then stopped. Cautiously, Joaquin peeked over the top of the arroyo. "It's them," he said. "Time to go."

The truck was half full of branches and clippings from shrubbery. The men climbed onto the truck and burrowed under the shelter that would hide them from *la migra*. There were so many of them that they had to form a double layer. The men on the bottom could barely breathe because of the pressure on their ribs.

Less than an hour later, soaked with perspiration and with every muscle aching, Alfredo was entering the back door of a "safe house" that was located just outside of Phoenix. "Now, I have kept my part of the bargain," Joaquin said. "The rest is up to you." With those words, he walked out the door and climbed into the Indians' truck. A moment later, he was gone.

The man who owned the safe house allowed his guests to stay there as long as they had the money to pay him his daily rent of $10. For this amount, they were given a mattress to sleep on plus one small meal a day. If the men wanted anything else, they had to wait for the teenaged boy who appeared at the front door every afternoon. For the right price, he brought them food and ran errands and provided information about the jobs that were available in Phoenix. One by one, the members of Alfredo's group

The Desert Will Bite You, Scratch You, or Poison You

ventured out onto the streets to take those jobs. And then, five days after Alfredo's arrival at the safe house, the boy announced that the fruit in the nearby orchards was ripening and that the ranchers were hiring pickers.

"Where are these ranches?" Alfredo asked.

"For five dollars, I will take you to a man who will hire you," the boy said.

Alfredo and several other men paid the boy's fee and climbed into the back of his pickup truck. Alfredo hoped the boy was telling the truth, because all he had left in his money packet was two dollars. Alfredo was afraid—afraid of being in a strange land with no money and no friends and no roof over his head.

His fear turned to relief when the boy stopped his truck along a country road many miles outside the city. "Here are your pickers," he called to an overalled man who was waiting beside a large flatbed truck.

"Good, I'll put them to work right away," the man replied.

Within an hour, Alfredo was on a ladder using special clippers to pick lemons from the endless rows of trees. By the end of the day, his hand muscles were throbbing with sharp pains, but the thought of the $1.50 he received for each eighty-pound bag of fruit he picked allowed him to look forward to the next day and the next and the next. As long as the lemons lasted, he would pick, because to return home would mean a return to the poverty in which his parents had spent their entire lives, the poverty which had caused the deaths of his two younger brothers while they were still infants.

THE UNCERTAIN JOURNEY

For dinner that evening, the workers were given bean burritos and cans of soda pop. After they had eaten, they talked for a while, then one by one they fell asleep in the bunks that were crowded into the barrackslike housing that had been provided for them.

After two years as a migrant farm worker, Alfredo was caught in an immigration sweep and, along with five other illegal aliens, was sent back to Guatemala on a commercial airliner.

"That plane ride was almost worth getting deported for," he says, grinning. "And besides, I was able to see my family again."

Alfredo stayed in his homeland for a month before making his second trip northward. This time he had enough money to buy a false travel visa which assured him an easy journey all the way to Tijuana, just below the California border. There, he hired a coyote to take him to Los Angeles, where he had arranged to meet some friends.

Since he had developed a severe allergy to many of the pesticides that were sprayed on farm crops, Alfredo decided to stay in Los Angeles and look for some other kind of work. He and another Guatemalan pooled their money, bought an old truck, and went into the recycling business. Every day, they park near a busy intersection and for eight hours sit and wait for people to bring bags and boxes of aluminum cans. Alfredo and his partner buy the cans for much less than they can sell them for at one of the central recycling centers.

Despite the fact that each man is sending $150 a month to his family in Guatemala, business is so good that they have saved almost enough money to buy another truck and set up shop at another street corner.

(LEFT) To pay his rent and buy food, this man pushes an ice-cream cart while the temperature hovers in the high nineties. Photo by Gary McCarthy.

(BELOW) Undocumented workers are often hired by the day to do construction work for home owners. Photo by Gary McCarthy.

Immigrant farm workers are often transported by truck from their camps to the fields. Photo by Gary McCarthy.

Modern technology hasn't replaced the time-honored horse patrol. Courtesy of the U.S. Immigration and Naturalization Service.

A combination of horse patrols and helicopters prevents the entry of many illegal aliens, but many more will slip across the border undetected. Courtesy of U.S. Immigration and Naturalization Service.

Bad luck! Hiding in a cover of brush didn't prevent three hopeful immigrants from being spotted by a helicopter pilot. Courtesy of U.S. Immigration and Naturalization Service.

Later, the three illegal aliens are led away to be taken back by bus to Mexico.
Courtesy of U.S. Immigration and Naturalization Service.

10

The Darkness Hides the *Banditos*

For Primo, the journey to the border of the United States was a short one: His home was a tar-paper shack on the hills near the Mexican city of Tijuana, which is within walking distance of the southern California border. His older brother, Raoul, had made many trips northward. Several times he had returned of his own volition to visit his family, twice he had been caught and deported by immigration officials. When Primo turned sixteen, he decided to join Raoul in Los Angeles. The five dollars an hour his brother made as a carpenter's helper was a fortune compared to the few dollars Primo made selling the salvage he found in the dumps near his home.

Primo knew the crossing of the border could be dangerous, but he was too impatient to wait for Raoul's next trip to Tijuana. After saying good-bye to his mother and his two younger brothers, he put a change of clothes and some bread and cheese into a large plastic bag. Late afternoon found him walking away from town, away from the border checkpoint, past the dumps and toward the brush-covered hills that lay between him and the border. Dusk found him sitting in an open area, along with dozens of other people who were waiting for the darkness that would hide their movements. A few feet away a woman was heating tortillas over an open fire, while a man strummed a guitar. Near the edge of the clearing, several children were tossing a ball back and forth.

A vendor moved from group to group, selling tamales and burritos from a large metal container, and a *coyote* offered safe transportation to San Diego and Los Angeles. Primo bought a tamale, but shook his head when the *coyote* approached him. In San Ysidro, across the border, Raoul would be waiting for him with a borrowed car, and, taking the back roads, would drive to Los Angeles.

As he waited, Primo tried to rest, but his mind was filled with the dangers that awaited him in the hills and gullies he was about to cross. Raoul had told him to watch out for the Mexican police whose job it was to prevent the crossing of the border, and about *la migra,* the officers who stood ready to turn the immigrants back as soon as they stepped onto the soil of *El Norte.* He had warned him about the slippery rocks and sand that caused people to fall over the sides of embankments and of the rattlesnakes that struck at unwary travelers.

And he had told him about the *banditos,* the thugs who robbed and beat and sometimes killed the men and women who were making their way to what they hoped would be a better life.

"Better to meet the Mexican police or *la migra,*" he had

THE UNCERTAIN JOURNEY

said. "You might have to bribe the police to let you pass, and *la migra* will send you back across the border, but they will not slice you with a knife or shoot you." Raoul himself had once been attacked by bandits. He was one of the fortunate ones: He lost his money, but he was not injured.

"The darkness that hides you from *la migra* also hides the *banditos*," Raoul had said. "Try to travel with others. In that way, you will not get lost and there will be less chance that you will be attacked."

Primo already knew that the man who was playing the guitar had made the trip across the border many times. His name was Juan, and he often acted as a *coyote,* providing *pollos* with transportation to California's Imperial Valley, where there was plenty of farm work. When Juan stood up and slung his guitar across his back, Primo also stood up, although the sun was not yet completely hidden from view.

Forty minutes later, Primo was making his way along a narrow trail that ran along the side of a steep rocky hill. By now, it was so dark that he had to walk no more than two feet behind the man in front of him. Left on his own, he would certainly have stepped off the trail and slid down the embankment, perhaps into a nest of rattlesnakes.

He reached the crest of the hill and started slipping and sliding down the gravelly pathway into a narrow gully that wound its way northward. Somewhere up ahead of him, a child cried out. He stumbled over an object, and when he looked down saw a small shoe and then a youngster's jacket, dropped and left there in the haste to get across the border.

The child was now quiet, but from the east, there came the sounds of gunshots. *Banditos,* Primo thought, looking over his shoulder, half expecting that a man with a knife would be coming up behind him. But he saw only the man and woman who had started this trek with him.

And then Primo heard another sound—that of the whirling blades of a helicopter hovering in the sky almost directly overhead. The beam of its searchlight swept the area that lay just the other side of the border, which was now only several hundred yards north of Primo and his companions. Everyone ducked down into the gully, trying to blend in with the shadows cast by the rising moon. Primo pressed himself into the ground, hoping to become invisible, feeling that if he moved a muscle, if he took a breath, the hovering monster in the sky would spot him, track him until he crossed the border, then with cruel talons reach down and pluck him from among all the other travelers who were crouched nearby.

A few moments later, the helicopter moved on, and Primo started to breathe again. Within seconds, the ghostly line of people began to move. Primo felt his way up and over another hill and across a marshy area. And there, at last, were the huge drainage pipes, one end of which lay in Mexico, the other of which lay in the United States.

Some of the pipes, or tubes, as they are commonly called, are big enough to allow a tall man to stand upright.

THE UNCERTAIN JOURNEY

Some are only three feet in diameter. They provide two advantages during a border crossing: The people inside are hidden from the border patrol, and the route is a fast one, ending in a busy suburb of San Diego where it is easy to get lost in the crowd. The disadvantage is that in the pitch darkness, the travelers find it hard to protect themselves from the thugs who may lie in wait for them halfway through the length of the pipe.

Primo planned to use a tube for his crossing. He and a group of men walked across the busy highway that runs parallel to the border, then dropped into a ditch. Suddenly, Primo saw a Mexican police car coming down the highway. He dropped face down in the ditch. With his nose buried in the dirt, he listened as the police questioned two of the men who had been following him.

He knew he would not be able to make it to the tube without being spotted. Like a furtive animal, in the faint light of the shadowed moon, he crawled from the ditch and under a ten-foot-high cyclone fence. Now he was in the dreaded Smugglers' Canyon, which was located just north of the border. The canyon, Raoul had told him, was like a minefield, filled with sensors placed there by the border patrol. Even worse, it was a hiding place for robbers and murderers, and Primo was now separated from the group he had been following.

He ran behind a clump of brush to catch his breath and to listen for the sound of jeeps and helicopters and to peer into the darkness for any signs of a thug lying in wait for him. When he saw or heard no indication that a border

The Darkness Hides the Banditos

patrol sensor had been set off, he joined another lone traveler who was passing by.

"We are almost to River Bottom, a dangerous place," said Primo's new companion. "Here, there are many who would hit you over the head whether you have money or not. And here *la migra* lies in wait."

The words had barely been spoken when Primo saw headlights boring into the darkness just ahead of them. The two men threw themselves behind a large bush, then rolled into a shallow ditch. Primo heard a car door slam, saw the sweep of a flashlight's beam, heard voices. "We know you're there," a border patrolman called in Spanish. "We saw you. Come on out."

Primo took a deep breath and made himself as flat as possible. He heard the sound of boots crunching the underbrush and the squawking of walkie-talkies. His heart was pounding so hard he was sure *la migra* would hear it above all the other voices of the night.

But ten minutes later, car doors slammed and the patrol car made its way past them up the winding road. Primo and his companion waited until the sound of the car had died out, then, crouching and stumbling, they climbed up the side of the canyon. According to what Raoul said, Primo figured it wouldn't be long before they reached the comparative safety of the highway. He took a deep breath, congratulating himself on the successful completion of his short but hazardous journey.

His congratulations were short-lived. Seconds later, there was the sound of brush being trampled underfoot.

THE UNCERTAIN JOURNEY

Primo barely had time to turn around to protect himself before he was thrown to the ground by two bearded men. Holding a knife to Primo's throat, one of the *banditos* snarled, "Give me your money, your watch, all your valuables." As he spoke, his free hand was digging in Primo's pockets, taking the few dollars that he found there. The other man grabbed Primo's plastic bag and dumped its contents onto the ground. When he found nothing of value, he picked up the clothing and slit it with his knife.

Don't kill me. Please don't kill me, Primo prayed silently. He moaned and curled up as one of his tormentors kicked him in the ribs. The *banditos* then pushed him off the side of the narrow trail into a shallow ravine, and, with raucous laughs, scrambled down the side of the canyon.

Primo lay at the bottom of the ravine for almost ten minutes. Every breath he took caused a sharp pain in his chest, and he hoped that none of his ribs was broken. When he was satisfied that the thugs would not return, he climbed back up to the trail, gasping and stumbling. He squinted at the darkness, hoping to see his companion, not daring to call out for fear the *banditos* would hear him and come back to kill him.

His companion had fled when the thugs attacked. Primo was alone. He had no money. His good clothes had been ruined. If he hadn't known that Raoul was at this moment waiting for him in San Ysidro, he might have turned around and gone back to the familiar streets of Tijuana. Squaring his shoulders, taking care not to take a deep breath, he climbed out of the canyon, then headed for the highway that lay to the west. Less than an hour later, he had met Raoul and was on his way to Los Angeles where, he hoped, his fortune would take a turn for the better.

Primo found that being in the section of downtown Los Angeles where he and Raoul lived with three other *sin papeles* was almost like being in Mexico. The streets were crowded with Spanish-speaking people. The billboards and business signs used Spanish words. There were Spanish newspapers and radio and television stations. Restaurants and grocery stores sold Mexican, Guatemalan, and Salvadoran food. Salsa and ranchero music could be heard everywhere along the crowded dirty streets.

Since it was the middle of summer, Primo took a job as an ice-cream vendor. Every day from noon until late in the evening, he walked through the nearby parks and the residential streets, pushing his cart with the small tinkling bell attached to the handle, stopping only to wait on customers and for a quick snack in the late afternoon. The more territory he covered, the more sales he could make and the faster he would be able to send some money to his mother. Once, though, in an isolated section of the park, he was set upon by a robber. The man had a gun, and Primo felt fortunate that he lost only a day's earnings and not his life.

In October, when the weather grew cool, fewer people wanted ice cream, so Primo found a job in a carwash and worked weekend evenings in a neighborhood grocery store. In February, he and Raoul enrolled in night school to study English. It was during the spring break from school that Primo went to a party given by Miguel, a friend of a classmate.

THE UNCERTAIN JOURNEY

Miguel had left Honduras when his first-born child, a daughter, died because he had no money to buy her the medicine she needed. He had left behind his wife and an infant son. After four years, during which he had set up a metal-working shop in the garage of his home, he was able to pay a *coyote* to bring his family to Los Angeles. Now they were reunited, and Miguel was hosting a party to celebrate their arrival.

Two months later, Primo went to work for Miguel on the weekends. As he learned how to work with metal, he began to dream about buying a metal lathe of his own. In Mexico, with such a machine, he could have all the work he wanted. He would never be poor again.

"Lathes cost thousands of dollars," Raoul said. "To help out, I will try to send more money home so you can save more."

"When I get the machine, why don't we become partners?" asked Primo. "We can both return to Mexico and I will teach you what I know."

Raoul wasn't certain about what to tell Primo. He had been in the United States long enough to apply for amnesty. Since he had learned to read and write English, he had become a leadman in the wire factory where he now worked. He had met a girl who was a citizen, and he was thinking about marrying her. If he could gain amnesty, he would be able to move freely back and forth across the border to see his family. There would be little advantage in making a permanent move back to Mexico.

"I'll let you know," he said. "With or without me, you will become a successful business owner."

─────── *The Darkness Hides the* Banditos ───────

* * *

During the next two years, Primo saved his money and learned all he could about his new trade. Three times he was picked up by *la migra* and transported back to Tijuana, and three times he was back in Los Angeles within a week. He didn't mind being deported, because he knew he would be able to return, but he did resent the time he lost from work. Every day's wages meant that much more money saved for his lathe.

Because of the constant possibility of being picked up by immigration officials, Primo, like many illegal aliens, usually carried at least one hundred dollars in his wallet. This money enabled him to buy food while he was in Mexico and to pay his bus or train fare back to Los Angeles. The same money, however, made him a tempting target for thieves. One night, on his way home, he was pulled into an alley and robbed at knifepoint. A month later, a pickpocket took his wallet.

To be a *sin papeles* is to be a victim, he thought. He didn't report the crimes to the police. What good would it do? The robbers would not be caught, and Primo would probably be reported to the immigration service.

"It just means it will be a little longer before I get my lathe," he told Raoul. Meanwhile, he kept the bulk of his savings in a safe place in his apartment. Primo felt that he was fortunate to have a trustworthy person taking care of his money whenever he was deported.

Primo had just begun his third year in *El Norte* when he took a night job in a restaurant as a clean-up man. It was

THE UNCERTAIN JOURNEY

here that he met Pablo, a forty-year-old man who lived in a small room located behind the office. Here, for five years, he had slept on a cot after finishing his double shift as a dishwasher. He ate all of his meals at the restaurant, seldom venturing outside, and then only late at night. If he needed razor blades or a new shirt, he paid one of the busboys to do his shopping for him.

This sallow-skinned man aroused Primo's curiosity. At first, Pablo was reluctant to answer any questions, but as the weeks passed, he seemed to welcome the chance to talk to someone. Primo learned that he was from Guatemala.

"You find it a simple thing to return after being deported," Pablo said. "For me, it would be the end of my dreams, because I would not have the strength to make that journey again. That is why I must stay in hiding, and why I am so grateful to my *patron,* who allows me to stay here. In just one more year, I will have enough money to buy a house and some land. Just one more year, and I will be able to feel the sun and the wind again." He pointed to the picture of his wife and three children. "Even better, I will be with my family."

Primo knew that long after he himself had reached his goal and returned to Mexico, he would remember Pablo sitting on his tattered cot in this tiny room. At those times, Primo would realize that the sacrifices he had made to make his dream come true were trivial compared to the sacrifices that Pablo had made.

Primo had saved almost four thousand dollars—one thousand less than he needed for a new metal lathe—when Miguel told him

The Darkness Hides the Banditos

about a secondhand lathe that was being sold by a factory owner.

"He's asking twenty-five hundred dollars, but you should offer him only two thousand," Miguel said. "I think he will let you have it for that price." By the end of the week, the deal had been struck. Now, Primo is arranging to have the lathe shipped to Tijuana, where he has rented a small building. Already, his seventeen-year-old brother has talked to several potential customers, and they are waiting for Primo to arrive so they can do business with him. Primo is grateful to El Norte *for giving him the chance he would never have had if he had stayed in Mexico.*

11

You Will Never Work as I Have Worked

"I must work or my children will starve." That was the desperate comment that Jeremiah made to a friend when he decided to go to the United States.

Jeremiah is from Jamaica, where he has a wife and three children. Although he finished primary school and can read and write, he could find no work, so he bought a small plot of land and became a farmer. It took him only a year to realize that the soil on his farm was too poor to raise a good crop. Hoping to make enough money to buy fertilizer to enrich his land, Jeremiah went to work on a banana plantation. Here he found that his wages barely covered the food and clothing his family needed. Three years later, he began cutting sugarcane. Since this work paid a little more, he was able to set some money aside with which to improve his land.

Jeremiah had been cutting sugarcane for only two seasons when one of his children, then another, became ill. Because of the cost of medical care, his savings were soon gone. And when the savings were gone, he could no longer pay for the medicine his children needed, and they both died. As he grieved for them, he vowed that he would not let poverty take any more members of his family.

"I will go to the United States," he said to his wife. "The men who go to the United States come back with new boots, plaid shirts, and gold watches and rings. Their children grow plump because they eat so well."

The next morning, Jeremiah went to a moneylender to borrow money for the trip.

"I am an honorable man," Jeremiah said. "I will pay you back."

The moneylender smiled. "I am not worried," he said.

Jeremiah knew by the coldness in his eyes that the moneylender had no reason to worry. If the debt were not repaid on time, he would not hesitate to seize Jeremiah's land. In such an event, Jeremiah's family would most certainly become homeless and might eventually starve. At the time, however, Jeremiah saw no other way of getting to the United States. Borrowing from this man was only the first of many risks he was certainly going to have to take. Still, he hesitated to sign the papers.

"Let me think about it," he said. "I will come back tomorrow."

The moneylender shrugged. "As you wish," he said.

Jeremiah's moment of hesitation turned out to be fortunate for him. As he walked back home that afternoon, he met a friend, a former sugarcane cutter who had grown too old to work in the fields.

THE UNCERTAIN JOURNEY

"I hear that sugarcane cutters are needed in Florida," the friend said.

"Yes, but I do not like to borrow so much money to make the journey," Jeremiah said.

"But you don't have to pay to go," said the friend. "Just be at the village square tomorrow morning. The town officials are looking for workers to send to the labor contractors. If you are chosen, the contractors will pay your way to the United States."

When Jeremiah arrived at the square at seven o'clock the next day, many other workers were already gathered there. Jeremiah knew that each of the men must be as poor as he himself was. Who else but a desperate man would freely offer to leave his home and family to travel to a foreign country to do the grueling dangerous work involved in cutting sugarcane?

Thirty minutes later, two town officials appeared and told the men to form a line. Each man wanted to be first, but there was little jostling as the order was obeyed. One by one, in turn, the men were questioned by the officials, who then inspected their hands to see if they bore the callouses and toughened skin that resulted from many seasons of hard labor. Jeremiah watched from his position halfway back in the line as the officials nodded their heads in acceptance or shook them in rejection. When he realized that only about half the men were accepted, his throat grew dry and his stomach tightened.

Finally he was at the head of the line. "Your name?" "Where are you from?" "Have you cut sugarcane?" "For how many years?" "How soon can you leave?" Jeremiah answered the questions as fast as they were asked. He held out his hands, palms up, when he was asked.

"Accepted," the officials said. "Wait over there with the others."

Jeremiah's relief was short-lived. He soon found that there would be another hurdle to overcome. The group that was accepted was to be sent to the capital city of Kingston to be inspected and questioned by the labor contractors. It was these men who would be making the final decision about who would go and who would be left behind.

In Kingston, Jeremiah found himself competing with men from many townships, but his work-toughened hands, his strong stature, and his experience in the sugarcane fields earned him a place among the fifty workers who were chosen.

The plane trip from the Kingston Airport to Florida lasted less than an hour. Jeremiah had barely enough time to adjust to the fact that he was actually in the United States before he and the rest of the workers were put onto a bus. Within two hours, the men were being led into a compound that was surrounded by barbed wire and guarded by bearded men with guns. Are they expecting us to try to escape? Jeremiah wondered. Or are they protecting us from the immigration officials? Whatever the answer, the presence of the guards made him uncomfortable.

The next morning before the sun rose, the clanging of a bell awakened Jeremiah. Within half an hour he had eaten a breakfast of grits and white bread and had joined the line of men who were being packed into trucks in which they rode to the fields.

For the next ten hours, Jeremiah swung a machete, stopping only twice, once to eat a cheese sandwich, another to line up for a drink of water ladled out from a barrel. His lungs were filled with the acrid smoke that rose from the burning leaves in the fields being prepared for harvest, but every time he stopped to cough, the crew leader yelled at him to get back to work. As he leaned over to chop the plants off at the roots, his back ached, but he dared not take the time to straighten up to ease the pain, and he dared not complain. The troublemakers, and the men who didn't meet their quotas, were sent back to Jamaica with no pay.

Each night the cutters were fed poorly prepared food. They joked about the small portions, saying that it tasted so bad they would never be able to stomach second helpings anyway. They then went to their barrackslike living quarters to try to get a few hours of sleep. The air in the building, which Jeremiah shared with a hundred other men, was stifling, and the bunks were placed so close together there was barely room to step between them. Sleep was sometimes a long time in coming. The heat pressed down upon him like a heavy blanket, and the snoring and moaning coming from the other men, plus the music from three or four radios, caused him to toss and turn until exhaustion overcame him.

There were times when the only thing that kept Jeremiah going was the thought of the two or three thousand dollars he could make during this one harvest season. Even after he paid for his room and board, there would be enough money to support his family for a year and to buy a better piece of land in Jamaica.

It was a series of accidents and close calls that caused Jeremiah to decide to leave the work crew. The flailing razor-sharp machete used in the cutting of sugarcane has inflicted many serious injuries even under the best of conditions. Since the men with whom Jeremiah worked were often exhausted from lack of sleep, and they were working under pressure, with high quotas to fill, injuries were commonplace. One of the men received a deep gash in his leg. Two days later, another worker lost part of his hand. The following week, a man who was picking up a bundle of stalks from the ground was struck in the back by the machete of a worker in the adjoining row. He was sent back to Jamaica to spend the rest of his life in a wheelchair.

Jeremiah was fortunate—the foot injury he received was minor, and after being bandaged he was able to return to work. Still, the experience caused him to wonder what would happen to his family if he was crippled. Better to take a chance on finding other work, he reasoned. That night, as he lay awake, he made his plans. Ordinarily, the cover of darkness makes an escape easier, but at night, armed guards patrolled the compound. He would have to take flight during the day, sometime when his crew leader's attention was drawn elsewhere and when the guards' backs were turned.

Two weeks later, just after payday, Jeremiah was working on the edge of the field. As he chopped and gathered the sugarcane stalks, he waited for a chance to dart unseen into the nearby woods. When the moment arrived, he was

THE UNCERTAIN JOURNEY

surprised at how easily he escaped. The only ones who noticed him leave were the men who had been working nearby, and they said nothing. That night, Jeremiah lay on the ground under a tree and had the first good night's sleep he'd had since coming to the United States.

Jeremiah spent two years following the Florida harvests. He picked melons, strawberries, oranges, lemons, and grapefruit. It was while he was harvesting tomatoes that he started thinking about making a change in his life. It was the last pick of the season and the crop was red-ripe and rotting on the vines. As he worked his way up and down the endless rows, gnats and flies buzzed around his face, forcing him to periodically pause to brush them away from his nose and eyes. At the same time, the muggy breeze swirled dust into his face and inside his shirt collar.

These annoyances were small compared to the unrelenting, oppressive midday heat that lay over the workers like a wet steaming blanket. Rivulets of sweat trickled from Jeremiah's forehead and seeped into his eyes. Mixed with the grime from the fields, it formed a film on any exposed part of his body.

Alternately pushing and dragging his basket, Jeremiah and the two hundred other workers squatted and crawled along the rows. A filled basket weighed between thirty or forty pounds. Toward the end of the day, many workers, especially the women, stumbled under the weight as they hoisted the cumbersome containers to their shoulders and carried them to the checker, who moved from row to row.

You Will Never Work as I Have Worked

For each basket, the checker handed the worker a ticket that would be worth fifty cents on payday.

Each time a worker turned in a filled basket, an empty one awaited him. Except for a lunch break and another short break, the work continued without pause. Only the crew leader was able to sit in the shade of a pine tree. His pants legs weren't torn and stained with insect spray. His hands and knees weren't scratched and bloody from encounters with rocks. His back didn't ache.

Why don't I become a crew leader? Jeremiah wondered. I can talk to the ranch owners. I've saved enough money to buy a bus. I've watched the way the crew leaders handle their business.

At that time, Jeremiah thought the job of being a crew leader was an easy one, but he was wrong. A crew leader must handle many tasks. It's his job to locate the growers that need help, then guarantee those growers that he can supply the necessary number of workers at the times they are needed. He is responsible for transporting the crews, whether the distance is only a few miles or halfway across the country. When they arrive at the work site, the crew leader must get the workers to the fields every morning, then take them back to their camp or housing quarters at night. He must keep order at those sites and settle any differences that might arise among the members of his crew.

While his workers are in the field, the crew leader must direct and oversee them. He keeps a record of how much money is owed to each worker, and on payday, gives them their wages. He is responsible for the behavior of his workers, both on the job and off.

A crew leader is paid in a variety of ways. Sometimes he is given a set amount—for example, fifty dollars for each day he delivers a crew to a field and supervises them. Sometimes, he receives a percentage of the value of the harvested crop. For instance, a crew leader could receive ten dollars for each two hundred buckets of tomatoes that are picked by one of his workers.

Since the crew leader is in business for himself, he must furnish his own trucks and buses and pay for all transportation costs. He must also pay for his workers' insurance and keep their Social Security records. When he is new in his job, he must be able to convince a grower that he is able to provide the correct number of workers on the days that they are needed and that he will be able to manage them while they are on the job. He must then convince a group of workers that he actually has work for them, that he won't cheat them on payday, and that he will give them decent housing and safe transportation.

For Jeremiah, the dream of becoming a crew leader grew slowly. He knew that it would mean either remaining separated from his family or illegally bringing them into the United States. The immigration authorities would be able to spot an entire family much more quickly than they would one person. And what if Jeremiah was deported and his family was left behind in the United States?

Also, depending on the vagaries of the weather, the market prices, and the labor supply, a crew leader could

You Will Never Work as I Have Worked

become poor as easily as he could become rich. At least as a picker, Jeremiah had always been able to send money home to his family and even save some.

Finally, although he was unsure of the wisdom of his decision, Jeremiah used his savings to buy an old bus, then drove from orchard to orchard seeking a contract with their owners. A week later, with a guarantee of work for his crew, Jeremiah drove to Miami to recruit workers from a group of newly arrived aliens. He picked his people carefully, hiring only those he felt were dependable and would not cause trouble.

Within three days, the members of his crew were picking fruit while Jeremiah strode back and forth along the rows of trees, encouraging the slower pickers, complimenting the faster ones.

"Each bag picked is a dollar and fifteen cents in your pocket," he said. And thirty cents for me, he thought. Already he was looking ahead to the time when he could buy another bus, hire more men, and make still more money. In the United States, anything was possible. He could even consider the possibility of hiring someone to bring his wife and children to Florida. Someday, he thought, I will be with my family again.

Two weeks before the last of the lemon crop was picked, Jeremiah drove a hundred miles north to an area where workers would soon be needed. After getting a contract from a tomato grower and renting a large old house where he and his workers could stay for the season, he drove back to pick up his crew.

For the next year, Jeremiah and his crew traveled around

THE UNCERTAIN JOURNEY

Florida and into Georgia and Alabama. Sometimes, when the work was plentiful, they were on the job twelve to fifteen hours a day, sleeping only a few hours to be up before the sun rose. Occasionally, when the crop began to thin out, Jeremiah told the workers to stop work at noon and get into the bus for a trip to town. There they ate chili and burritos and hamburgers, then went to a movie or an amusement park, returning to their housing site long after dark to sleep late the next day. For Jeremiah, his crew took the place of the family and friends he had had to leave behind in Jamaica.

Another year passed, and Jeremiah had saved almost enough money to either buy another bus or to bring his family into the United States. He decided he wanted to be reunited with his family more than to expand his business. Two months later, he drove to Miami for a joyful meeting with his wife and children.

"You have not changed at all," he said to his wife, then he turned to his children. "But you have changed—so tall, so different from what I remember." He led them to his bus. "Get in. We haven't too far to travel."

On the way to the grapefruit orchards where his men were to begin working the following week, Jeremiah's wife told him about her trip while his children silently stared at him. However, after he stopped and bought them hamburgers and ice cream, they seemed to accept him, and the bus was filled with their chatter and laughter.

"I can help pick the fruit," said his fifteen-year-old son. "I can help too," echoed his twelve-year-old daughter.

You Will Never Work as I Have Worked

"No, I will not have you working in the fields," said Jeremiah. "You will go to school. You will become teachers and lawyers. You will never work as I have worked."

It wasn't long before Jeremiah's order to his children had to be temporarily set aside. Early one morning during the second week of the new contract, the cry of "Immigration! Immigration!" scattered the members of his crew as they started their day's work. Fleeing in every direction, they hid in drainage ditches and in shrubbery, but almost half of them were in the hands of immigration officials by the end of the day. The next morning, Jeremiah and his entire family were pressed into service. Even his six-year-old son was put to work picking up the older fruit that had fallen to the ground and which could be sold to a juice processing plant. Everyone started work just as the sun rose and didn't stop until it was so dark they could no longer see.

As the weeks passed, Jeremiah was able to hire more men from among the illegal aliens who prowled the fields and orchards looking for work, and a few of his original crew managed to make their way back to Florida after having been transported to Mexico by the immigration service. Right on schedule, he managed to fulfill his contract and was paid in full by the woman who had hired him.

Because of Jeremiah's nomadic life-style, his children have not yet been able to attend a school for more than a few months at a time. To offset this disadvantage, Jeremiah has hired a tutor who travels with them from work site to work site. They now read and write fluently, and their grades compare favorably with those of the best students in the various schools they attend.

THE UNCERTAIN JOURNEY

Jeremiah has bought his second bus and now supervises fifty workers. His wife has learned to keep the payroll and Social Security records. She also occasionally treats their workers to a lunch or a dinner of Jamaican dishes.

Jeremiah was in the United States before the amnesty deadline. He has taken the required classes and passed the tests and completed all the paperwork and is now waiting for the document that will say he is a legal resident of the United States. The only cloud hanging over his head is the fact that his wife and children are still in danger of being deported. He has consulted an attorney who specializes in the problems of illegal aliens and is hopeful that within a year his family will be given permanent resident's status.

12

I Want to Help You

The sky above the desert was pitch black, relieved only by the sliver of a new moon and the pinpoints of light from a myriad of stars. There was a brief whistle from beyond the rise, followed by the blink of a flashlight. The way was clear; it was safe to proceed. Shadowy figures materialized from the darkness of the night to gather in a circle near a little-used Arizona highway.

Candido, from Honduras, had paid a *coyote* fifteen hundred dollars to gain him entry into the United States. Now, he was on the last leg of a journey that had taken almost three weeks. He and twenty other *sin papeles* would soon be in California.

Without speaking, the leader of the group snapped his fingers and started the trek toward the next scheduled pick-up point. The men spent the next five hours walking almost thirty miles, which to most of them was nothing more than a brisk stroll. At the end of that time, they boarded the old bus which was to take them to San Diego.

THE UNCERTAIN JOURNEY

Here, they had been told, there was work for all of them. Here, they could make their long-held dream of being part of *la vida Americana* become a reality.

It took Candido only two weeks to find a job, but six months later, he was far from living the good life he had envisioned before he came to *El Norte*. He spent ten hours a day, six days a week, in a car wash using an old rag to dry the cars after they had been through the cleaning machines. His pay consisted only of the tips he received from some of the customers: On a good day, he made ten dollars. Taking advantage of the fact that Candido was an illegal alien, his employer paid him no salary; in fact, his name was not even on the employment records of the company's books. Also, he gave Candido no time during the day to eat lunch or even to take a short break.

Candido felt that what his employer was doing was wrong, but he dared not complain. Aliens who had been able to apply for amnesty and had received temporary work permits had come out of hiding and were taking the better-paying jobs. For the hundreds of thousands of illegal aliens such as Candido, often the only work they could now find was from dishonest employers who underpaid and mistreated them.

Despite the poor working conditions, Candido had to keep his job so he could earn enough money to buy food and other necessities. He paid no rent, because he was living in a squatters' camp with a group of Mexicans who also worked at the car wash. This camp was in a canyon located just north of the city of San Diego where almost one hundred aliens had built shelters from cast-off lumber, plastic, and tin. As they washed their clothes in a polluted stream, the residents of the expensive homes in the surrounding hills were swimming in their heated pools. As they walked the six miles through the chapparal into the city to find work, they could see people hitting balls on the well-kept lawns of the golf course.

But there were no complaints from the camp residents. They were grateful to be with their friends and were comfortable in their little community.

One day in April, a young woman stood and watched Candido until he had a few minutes in which there were no cars to wipe down. As he gulped down a candy bar he carried in his pocket, the woman walked up to him.

"I'm a social worker with the county of San Diego," she said, showing him a business card with an official-looking seal on it. "I'd like to talk to you about your work here."

"No Engliss." Candido turned away, unwilling to talk to anyone connected with the government. He turned back when the woman started speaking Spanish.

"I want to help you. I believe you are being cheated by your employer," she said.

It's a trick, Candido thought. She cannot be trusted. *"No comprendo,"* he said. "No unnerstan'." Another car was coming down the line. He picked up his rag, wishing that the pesky woman would leave him alone.

But the social worker persisted. She was waiting around the corner when his shift was over. "Now, no one will see you talking to me," she said. "Your boss will know nothing about our conversation." She pulled a small notebook from her purse. "How much does he pay you for an hour's work?"

Candido decided that if he answered her questions, she would go away and leave him alone. "*Nada*. Nothing."

"What about breaks? How long does he give you to eat lunch?"

"No lunch. No breaks," Candido walked faster, but the woman stayed beside him.

"How many hours a day do you work?"

"Sometimes more, sometimes less. Usually ten or twelve."

"You have no green card, isn't that right?"

La migra, Candido thought. He tensed, prepared to flee.

"Don't run," the woman said. "I know you had a hard time finding this job, and you don't want to give it up. But your employer is not treating you fairly. You may be an undocumented worker, but that does not mean he can ignore the minimum wage law." She paused. "I'm not telling you to give up your job. I'm telling you that you have rights even if you are in this country illegally. I'd like to see to it that you get the back wages that are coming to you."

Four dollars an hour—that's the minimum wage, Candido thought. Ten hours a day, six days a week, for six months. He could not figure the amount in his head, but knew he could receive thousands of dollars. Even if he lost his job—even if he was deported—that amount would be worth his journey to *El Norte*.

"Yes," he said, smiling at the young woman. "I will answer your questions."

―――――― *I Want to Help You* ――――――

* * *

Only one week later, Candido was fired. Since he had done nothing wrong, he knew he had lost his job because he had been seen talking to the social worker. At first, he was angry at the woman: If she had minded her own business, he would still have a job. Then he was angry at himself: If he hadn't been so blinded by the idea of receiving so much money, he would not have cooperated with her. His boss would not have seen him answering all those questions. But he spent only one day cursing his luck and trying to find someone to blame. He had a better way to spend his energy. He had to find a job. Every day for over a month, he walked to town, stopping at businesses along the way to see if they needed help, asking the farmers in the fields if they could give him a few hours of work. But by the end of the month, he had worked a total of only six days.

One evening, as he and the other camp residents were heating their beans and tortillas over open fires, a van came over the hill and down into their canyon. The residents who had work permits stayed where they were. Candido and the other *sin papeles* ran into the brush, scattered, and hid in gullies and amid clumps of trees. They did not come out for half an hour, when one of the documented workers gave them the "all clear" signal. The news that awaited them was good, not bad.

"There's a new hiring site in San Diego," they were told. "Tomorrow, a bus will come to pick us up to take us there. The county worker said that we will be able to sign

THE UNCERTAIN JOURNEY

up for different sorts of jobs, and that some people will even teach us English and help us to get green cards."

"But what about *la migra?*" Candido asked.

"No problem—that's what the social worker said. And what if they do show up? We'll just run and get lost in the crowds."

The following morning, Candido and fifty other camp dwellers lined up to board the bus that appeared at 5:30. Many of the waiting men and women were suspicious. "It might be *la migra* playing a trick on us," one man said.

"Yes, perhaps we should walk to town," said another man. "This bus may be headed straight to Tijuana." He laughed. "No problem. We'll soon be back."

Candido and the other people in line needed jobs so desperately that they were willing to take almost any chance. When the bus pulled out, they were all on board.

The hiring site, called *el proyecto* (the project), was located in a small park in northern San Diego. Tables had been set up, and when each worker registered, he was asked to describe the type of job he wanted—masonry, roofing, gardening, factory work, construction work, fish cleaning and packing, washing cars.

"Anything," Candido said. "I will do anything. Here I have washed cars, but back home, I worked on a banana plantation, and for a while I worked in a silver mine. I am strong. I learn quickly."

"I'll put you down for farm work and gardening, and also for hauling and construction and factory work," said the woman who took the information from him. "We're here from six until noon Monday through Saturday, so you keep coming back until you find a job. And you can also register for English classes. Learning the language will help you in many ways."

After inquiring about the English classes, Candido spent the rest of the morning waiting to be hired by the contractors and other employers who came to the hiring site seeking workers. For the next two weeks, he boarded the bus every morning and returned home in the afternoon with no job but with an increasing knowledge of English. Each night, he ate his meager supper, hoping that the next day would bring him the work he prayed for every night.

But no job was offered to him. At the beginning of the third week, Candido became a street vendor, spending his afternoon hours sitting on an upended plastic milk crate on a street corner near San Diego's Old Town. He had purchased his cassette tapes, costume jewelry, and knickknacks from a traveling wholesaler and had priced them to make a small profit. Street vending was illegal, but as long as Candido wasn't caught, he could make twenty dollars a day. That was enough to buy food and to repay the small amounts of money he had borrowed from a few of the camp residents.

It was a long way from Candido's dream of *la vida Americana,* but he was content.

It was only three weeks later that his contentment was shattered. Since the police had confiscated his supply of trinkets and jewelry early in the afternoon, Candido walked back to the camp, grateful that he hadn't been arrested. As he approached the canyon, he smelled smoke

THE UNCERTAIN JOURNEY

and heard people shouting. Rounding a bend in the path, he saw flames leaping from one dwelling to another and from dry bush to dry bush. Candido ran to the stream and joined the frantic men who were filling buckets with water. Despite their efforts, by the time the fire department arrived, the flames had already destroyed almost the entire camp, including the hut that Candido had shared with two other men. Fortunately, since it was the middle of the day and most of the residents were at work, no lives were lost and there were only a few minor injuries.

After the firemen had left, the camp residents started picking through the sodden ashes, hoping to find some of their possessions that hadn't been completely destroyed. Candido searched for his Bible, which contained pictures of his family in Honduras. And there it was, charred and damp, but salvageable. One of his roommates searched in vain for the two thousand dollars he had saved for his journey home. The other roommate lost his valuable immigration documents. Some residents lost the bicycles they depended upon for transportation. Almost all lost their blankets, their clothing, and treasured mementos of the families they had left behind.

That night, there was no laughter or singing as Candido and his friends sat around a campfire. There was only subdued talk about the losses everyone had suffered. "It wasn't much, but it was all I had," one man said. "I had saved every letter from home," said another. "Now they are gone." "Bad luck," said a third man, who was standing beside the burned hulk of an old car he had bought for one hundred dollars. Candido was silent. He had no money, no job, no roof over his head. It was no better than being in Honduras.

And then someone mentioned that he knew where there was some scrap lumber. And someone else said that his boss was giving away some pieces of sheet metal. And Candido looked at the sky. It was clear. The weather was warm. It would not be so bad to sleep under the stars. And in the *Estados Unidos,* there was something that was missing in Honduras. Here, at least, there was hope.

"We face many hardships during our adventure in this country," he said. "But we will endure."

"Did you ever think we wouldn't?" asked one of his roommates. Candido laughed. Soon, there was more laughter, and the sound of ranchero songs filled the air.

The fire that had seemed so tragic at the time turned out to be a fortunate event for the people who lived there. A story in the local paper made the citizens of San Diego aware of the plight of the camp dwellers. Within two days, a church had donated a dozen plastic and wood sheds, each of which could shelter ten campers. The owner of a lumberyard donated wood, and the owner of a hardware store gave tools and nails and other building materials. The employers of some of the camp residents took up a collection and bought food. Three weeks after the fire, the members of the city's housing commission voted to give the campers ten thousand dollars to be used for emergency transportation, food, blankets, and clothing. No one could replace the documents and letters and pictures that had been burned, but because of the fire, the dwellings in the

THE UNCERTAIN JOURNEY

new camp would be stronger and more comfortable than any of the rickety, leaky structures that had stood there for the last three years.

There was never any doubt that the camp would be rebuilt, if not in that exact spot, then over the next rise. As one of the residents said, "Where else can we go?"

The atmosphere in the canyon was almost festive as the men spent their spare time erecting the new shelters. There was singing and joking, and during an occasional break, there was a soccer game in a charred field nearby. From a catering truck, a woman sold burritos and soft drinks and packages of potato chips. Volunteers came from the surrounding area to help. Some of them offered work to the camp residents. A reporter later wrote, "Maybe the help they received after the fire brought a little bit of new hope. Any time you're down as low as they were, you reach a point where you can't go down any further, and you have to look upwards."

Two weeks after the camp was rebuilt, Candido reported to the hiring site. He was met by the social worker who had asked him so many questions about his job at the carwash and who, Candido believed, had been the cause of his being fired.

"I've been looking for you," the woman said. "Just the other night I thought maybe you'd be registered here, and sure enough, your name was on their list."

"What do you want with me?" Candido asked. "Your questions brought me nothing but trouble."

"But it also brought you this." The woman smiled as

I Want to Help You

she handed Candido an envelope, which he opened. Inside was a check with his name on it. The check was for the amount of seven thousand dollars.

"So much money," Candido said. "Where did it come from?"

"Those are the wages that the owner of the car wash should have given you," the woman said.

"So much money," was all that Candido could say. Just a short time ago, he had no job and no money and no roof over his head. And now he had seven thousand dollars! Surely, this could happen only in the *Estados Unidos*.

Candido is now making plans to return to Honduras. He has not yet decided whether to buy a small farm or to buy a taxicab and go into business for himself. Since there is little public transportation in his hometown, he knows he could make a good living from the tourists who frequent the area.

"I'll probably become a taxi driver," he says. "That will make me a person of some importance among my friends. And never again will I be cheated by a *patron*."

I Have Survived!

For three decades, the illegal alien situation has been discussed at length by legislators, cabinet members, and presidents. Most of these discussions are based upon research that has been done by sociologists, educators, and economists. This research yields the facts and figures that indicate the impact that millions of undocumented workers have on our society.

These studies are valuable, but only a few of them begin where such studies should begin—with the *sin papeles* themselves. Because they are reluctant to talk to strangers, little is known about the people about whom so many words have been written and so many statistics compiled.

Now we have met some of these men and women. We have read of the hopeless poverty into which they were born and the risks and hardships they endured to escape that poverty. We have learned how some of them suffered persecution in their homelands. We have seen how their

I Have Survived!

energy and expectations enabled them to overcome the obstacles that they faced in a strange country and how their ambition drove them to succeed far beyond mere survival.

It's apparent that there are many similarities between today's illegal immigrants and the European immigrants who came here during the 1800s and 1900s. For both groups, the United States was and is a powerful magnet, an irresistible land of opportunity. Like the earlier immigrants, today's *sin papeles* want nothing more than a chance to earn a living.

Unlike the earlier immigrants, though, the *sin papeles* must live in hiding, knowing that, at any moment, they could be deported. Most of them are fortunate: The first time they cross the border they manage to find work and to avoid detection. Some are not so lucky: They must try again and again. Pedro, a Mexican, is embarrassed, but not discouraged, when he talks about his experience as a *sin papeles*.

"I was deported by *la migra* in Utah. The same thing happened in Detroit. Each time, I went back to *El Norte*. Then, in Phoenix, I made a wrong turn into a one-way street and was arrested. The police called the immigration office, and I was sent home again. All these things happened before I ever found a job!

"But *que sera, sera*. What will be, will be. Crossing the border is, after all, a gamble. Sometimes things don't work out. Next year, after I pay my debts, I'm going to take the trip again."

Pedro knows that if he keeps trying, eventually his luck

THE UNCERTAIN JOURNEY

will change. *La migra*'s eyes will be closed when he passes by. He will find a job. He may even be as successful as Francisco, Alicia, Arnulfo, and all the others whose lives are better because they took the necessary risks.

At that time, he will finally be able to say, *"Me defendi en la lucha.* I have survived the uncertain passage."

BIBLIOGRAPHY

Cockcroft, James. *Outlaws in the Promised Land.* New York: Grove Press, 1986.

Haskell, Grace. *The Illegals.* New York: Stein and Day, 1978.

Kessner, Thomas, and Betty Caroli. *Today's Immigrants.* Oxford: Oxford University Press, 1982.

Santoli, Al. *New Americans.* New York: Viking, 1988.

Wambaugh, Joseph. *Lines and Shadows.* New York: Morrow, 1984.

Wright, Dale. *They Harvest Despair.* Boston: Beacon Press, 1965.